DADDY'S WHIP

LOKI RENARD AND KELLY DAWSON

FOR AUDIENCES 18+ ONLY

This book is intended for adults only. Spanking and other sexual activities represented in this book are fantasies only, intended for adults.

CHAPTER ONE

Marnie put some toast in her mouth and turned the volume on her headphones up. It was a sunny Tuesday afternoon, and she had nothing planned but chilling out and playing on the internet for the rest of the day. She'd been at work all morning, blogging up a storm and it was time to relax.

A little wobble made her Milo slosh in the mug. She must have knocked the desk accidentally with her knee. She took a sip to lower the level and put the cup back down.

Boom!

The world shattered and started to unwind itself around her. The house swayed and creaked as the earth began to twist and tear. *Earthquake.* The word slammed itself into her head. She'd been in dozens of them before, rumbles and grumbles that made the lights sway and maybe dislodged a few loose objects. This was a different animal. It was a beast rising from the bowels of the earth, unleashing pure hell and a primal terror that ripped the facade of civilization aside in a second and left her staring at the vicious nature of reality.

Her Milo became a milky brown spray across the room, the closet burst open, showering the floor with shoes and clothes, her books flew off the shelves and then the bookcase itself toppled over on top of them. The world was in motion, everything flying this way and that.

Under the desk, or in the doorway.

Growing up in New Zealand, she'd been drilled on what to do in an earthquake since she was a very little girl. As she was being shaken like a pebble in a tin can, Marnie tried to make it to the door. It was only half a metre away, but it may as well have been a kilometre. There was no way she was getting to it. Her feet couldn't move on the shifting ground, the carpet jamming itself up and down against her as she swayed back and forth, staggering in place.

The shaking intensified. She could hear the cupboards flying open in the kitchen, glass smashing as jars of pasta sauce, cups, saucers, plates all propelled themselves through the air. This was it. She was going to die. She was going to fucking die in her pyjamas with half a bite of toast in her mouth and a podcast playing unabated. She didn't have time to cry, she didn't even have time to scream. Her mouth was dry, her teeth clenched hard together as she battled to survive what felt like the very end of the world.

And then it stopped. Or at least slowed. She couldn't tell if it was still shaking because now she was shaking from head to toe, her body flooded with absolute adrenaline. She ran for the door, heading for outside.

Never go outside.

Her body didn't give a damn about the official guidelines. Her body wanted to be out, away from the scary shaking. She sprinted out onto the footpath, where she found the ground moving beneath her feet, hard concrete waving up and down in slow undulations, like standing atop water. In the garden beyond, geysers of liquid sand were spurting from below, covering grass and burying flower beds in a matter of minutes. Later on, the news would call it liquefaction. In that moment, all she could say was *holy fuck*. Holy. Fuck. Over and over again.

Shocked and stunned, she hugged her arms around herself. How could this be happening? This wasn't an area known for active fault lines. Wellington, that's where the big one was supposed to happen. Not Christchurch. Christchurch was supposed to be safe.

But that didn't stop her neighbour's chimney from being on top of their car. And it didn't stop their kids from screaming and crying, and it didn't stop water from flooding up from nowhere and turning the street into a wet sandy mess, great holes opening up in the roads and pavements, houses suddenly sunk into the ground up to their windows.

Other people were coming out of their houses. She saw the same shock and pale fear on their faces as the ground rumbled again. Their suburb was adjacent to the central city, where clouds of smoke and dust were rising. It was the middle of the day and the city would have been packed.

Marnie tried to call her mum, but her fingers were suddenly too awkward to work the cell phone, and there wasn't any signal anyway. They'd been cut off. There was nothing. Nothing. Fuck.

"Are you okay?" A woman touched her shoulder. Marnie nodded, holding back sudden tears, and the lady, whose name she didn't know, ushered her over to where her family was gathered. Over the next little while, huddled groups of people formed in gardens and on the side of the road. Nobody wanted to be indoors if another one hit. Neighbours who never talked to one another in years suddenly became instant friends, bringing out cups of tea from their broken houses, finding camping equipment to put to good use. The news, spoken in hushed tones, was not good.

Buildings were down. People were inside.

That was the day Marnie learned you could feel death in the air. It was a stillness, a hollow feeling that resonated with some deep part of her, the core of what it meant to be human and part of a community. She'd never noticed it before. Only now that so much had been destroyed could she suddenly feel the web of humanity all around her, and the gaping holes where something and someone had suddenly become nothing and no one.

The earth kept rolling all night and into the next day. Every few minutes it would rumble and shudder again and adrenaline spiked through her as she anticipated the return of the beast. Over the following week, three hundred and sixty aftershocks rocked the broken city, and in the end, Marnie fled.

CHAPTER TWO

Two weeks later...

The bus rumbled, jolting Marnie out of her dozing sleep. She shuddered and opened her eyes. Every now and then, her mind would flash a vision of the world shuddering again. These pleasant green paddocks, her brain made them crack and fill with sand. There wasn't an up and a down anymore, and sometimes she thought it might just open up beneath her and she would fall forever.

Pushing her hands beneath her butt, she sat uncomfortably as the bus rumbled on. She hadn't seen anything resembling civilization for a while now. It was all paddocks with cows and sheep and the odd horse. It was supposed to be relaxing, but it was just a bit weird. She was used to clogged roads and cars all over the place, merging with little to nothing in the way of notice.

The bus was slowing down, though she wasn't sure why. Maybe there was something wrong with it. Or maybe they were picking a sheep up or something.

"This is your stop."

"Huh?" It took her a second to realize the driver was talking to her.

It didn't look like a stop. It was just a post on a dirt road. The driver was looking at her expectantly though, so she grabbed her bag, thanked him, and got off.

There wasn't anybody there to meet her. Her aunt had told her that someone called Sam would be there but as she looked around, it was clear that she was totally alone.

The bus driver put the bus into gear and trundled off into the distance. Hell. Marnie pulled out her phone, intending to call the place she was supposed to be staying, but there was no service. This place was a dead zone in almost every sense. A small herd of cattle in a nearby paddock began ambling over toward her, licking their noses, sticking their tongues into one nostril and then the other, basically picking their noses like school kids.

"Gross," she lectured the black and white beasts.

They didn't take her criticism on board.

"This whole place is gross," she complained, waving her hand in front of her face as a pair of copulating flies buzzed past.

A cloud of dust heralded a car coming down a road running parallel to the one the bus had come down. It drew closer and closer, turning into a dusty red Ford ute that pulled up to the bus post. She'd wandered a few metres away, but turned and looked as a guy got out.

He was wearing a blue check shirt and jeans with dirty knees. His boots were brown and covered in dust and dirt and probably some other stuff that didn't bear thinking about. When he got closer, she saw that he was cute, in a farmer sort of way. He had dark brown hair, shaggy around his ears, and bright blue eyes. He had stubble around his chin. He looked like he had a good few years on her twenty-two, maybe thirty or so. He had some smile lines around his eyes, though he wasn't smiling now.

"Marnie Sawyer?" He said her name in a rough rumble that was more like a statement than a question.

She lifted her head and glared at him. "Took you long enough."

• • • • • • •

She was cute, but she had a hell of an attitude on her.

Sam had just recently taken over Terako Treks from his aunt and uncle, who had sent him out to pick up the city kid they'd agreed to take on as an extra hand as a favour to some relative of hers. He hadn't thought much of it when they first told him. Everyone knew how devastating the earthquakes had been. He didn't blame anyone who wanted to get as far away from them as possible and Terako could always do with an extra pair of hands.

He was starting to get the sense that this pair of French tip manicured hands might be more trouble than they were worth. The girl hadn't dressed for the situation for starters. She was wearing a tank top that didn't offer any protection from the sun, short shorts that basically invited thistles and gorse to stick her thighs, her strappy shoes were a broken ankle waiting to happen, and he didn't care for the sneer on her lipstick-smeared mouth either.

"Sorry," he said. "Got here soon as I could."

She looked at him with a stony, unimpressed expression. "You shouldn't leave people waiting. It's hot out here."

It wasn't often that Sam's palms started itching within seconds of meeting a girl, but they were practically burning.

"Hold on," he said. "You can't have been here that long, I saw the bus when I was coming up."

"Should have been here to meet me," she said. "Not very good service."

"I'm not here to service you, brat," he growled before he could stop himself. "You're here to work."

She looked stunned, as if nobody had told her about that part of the deal. "I'm here to what?"

"This is a working farm. We run horse treks. You're familiar with horses, right?"

"I know what a horse looks like," she said, shrugging her shoulders. "That help?"

"You know what one looks like?" Sam snorted in disgust. "Well done." His voice dripped with sarcasm, but the brat standing in front of him didn't appear to notice. She was too busy looking down her nose at the dust covering his ute to realize that he was unimpressed by her immaculately styled, expensive haircut, and seriously wondering why he'd even bothered to come. This chick was going to be useless, he was sure of it.

"Chuck your bag on the back and get in," he told her gruffly. "It's too hot to stand around out here all day and I've got work to do."

She looked a little scared and backed away and he instantly felt sorry for her. Until she opened her mouth.

"Nuh-uh." She shook her head. "My bag's not touching that filthy thing. It will be ruined!"

"Well, there's no room for it inside the cab with us, so unless you want to leave it on the side of the road I don't see how you've got much choice."

She just stood there, staring in horror at the ute. He flexed his hands, wanting nothing more than to reach across and slap her disobedient ass.

"Hurry up," he growled, "before I do it for you."

When she didn't immediately comply, he took hold of her over-full bag, wrenched it free from her grasp, and flung it none too gently onto the tray of the ute before taking hold of her arm just above the elbow.

"Ow! You're hurting me!" she protested, trying to pull away. He held her firm.

"I'll be hurting you a lot more in a minute," he mumbled, only half under his breath as he steered her toward the passenger door of the ute. She didn't fight him like he'd expected her to, but neither did she cooperate. Not really. She did drag her feet toward the ute as he propelled her along, but it was the jerky movement of someone who was doing something mostly against their will.

Sam yanked the door open with one hand while keeping a firm grip on the city chick with the other. If he didn't assist her into the vehicle they could be here all day, and he didn't have all day to waste.

"Get in." It was an order, not a suggestion, but clearly it wasn't an order she was inclined to obey. She stood there on the side of the road looking forlornly in the direction she'd come from, completely ignoring the fact that he wanted to get going.

"Get in!" He raised his voice this time and added a snarl, and although she turned to him, she still didn't move.

He had no doubt that the glare she gave him was supposed to intimidate him into leaving her alone, but it didn't work. He'd been glared at by far scarier people than the sassy woman whose arm he still held. So instead of cowering, he returned a glare of his own; a fierce frown that warned most people they'd better obey, or else.

"Are you going to get in or would you rather stay here on the side of the road by yourself? Just FYI, we're in the middle of nowhere. That bus has long gone. The nearest house is miles away. If you're lucky, a car might go past in about an hour. No guarantees they'll stop for you, though." He let go of her arm and shrugged. "But suit yourself."

Leaving her standing exactly where she was, Sam walked around the back of the ute with brisk strides, intent on leaving no matter what the new trek assistant did. Aunt Magda would have his guts for garters if he turned up without her, but that couldn't be helped. There was work to do, and he was the only one around—well, him and this new assistant—to do it. But he breathed a sigh of relief as she swung into the passenger seat just before he opened his own door.

As Sam settled himself into the driver's seat he watched his sullen, silent passenger out of the corner of his eye. Her whole body bristled with tension and her nose was turned up in disgust as she gingerly took hold of the seat belt and buckled up. She clearly wasn't used to dirt; that was for sure.

He flexed his hands again. She was cute, but right now, she was acting like a totally spoiled brat.

• • • • • •

Marnie settled back into her seat and closed her eyes. Every time the ute bumped and jolted over the pot-holed road she felt sick. But after a few minutes she opened them again; closing her eyes hadn't helped like she thought it would. All it did was trick her mind into thinking she was back in Christchurch, back in the earthquake, as the ground rocked and rolled beneath her feet.

She looked out the window. They were heading toward the mountain range, the towering majestic Southern Alps with snow still visible at the very tips. She'd never been a mountain person. She'd always preferred concrete suburbia to the wilderness, and couldn't live without cell phone reception and decent WiFi. Would any of that even be available where they were going? And where *were* they going, exactly?

Bracing herself against the door, Marnie squirmed uncomfortably. The ute had definitely seen better days. Her bum was already numb from the long bus journey and now a spring poked into her relentlessly, no matter how many times she shifted position. No matter how she sat, it hurt. Either the loose spring was jabbing into her butt or it ached from being sat on for so long.

"How much further?"

"Not far."

Sam didn't take his eyes off the road when he responded to her question, very unhelpfully, she thought. Why did he have to be so vague? All he'd done so far was order her about and not tell her anything useful.

But he was definitely hot. Unhelpful and bossy, but hot. His hands were huge. The back of the one wrapped around the gearstick was work-roughened and though she couldn't see his palm, the calluses on the edges of his fingers suggested the rest of it would be tough and hard too, like sandpaper. His shirt sleeves were rolled to his elbow

10

exposing sinewy tanned forearms, muscular and strong.

Who was this guy anyway? Was he meant to be her boss? He'd said something about her being there to work, but she didn't know anything about that. Actually, now that she thought about it, she didn't know very much about her current situation at all. Her aunt had told her, probably in great detail, but she hadn't been listening. She'd been so traumatized from the earthquake and so desperate for a fresh start away from the city that she hadn't really cared where she went, as long as the ground stayed solid beneath her feet.

Her gaze travelled along Sam's arm to his shoulder. The muscles in his neck were tense, partially hidden by his shirt. He was badly in need of a haircut. He could look quite sophisticated if his overgrown mop was tamed and shaped instead of sitting on his collar. She frowned at the stubble darkening his jaw. Ordinarily she liked stubble, but this wasn't the designer stubble she was used to, with precision shaving shaped to emphasize a masculine jaw, making him look sexily rough around the edges. This was just plain unshaven. Personal grooming clearly wasn't high on his list of priorities.

Peering closer, she wrinkled her nose in distaste at the fine layer of dust coating his clothing and skin. Wherever he was taking her, if it was going to be as dusty as he was, she didn't think she wanted to go.

A green tin mailbox flashed by on her left as the ute slowed down just enough to slide into the road on the right and clattered too fast over a cattle grid, making her bones rattle. Biting her lip to smother her squeal, Marnie clutched at the door, terrified. She'd been shaken around enough over the past two weeks; all she wanted to do now was stay still. She wanted to sit on something that didn't wobble and stand on something that didn't sway. And she most definitely did not want to be tossed sideways in an out-of-control ute fishtailing around a corner on a gravel road.

"I want to go home." She hadn't meant to say the words

out loud, but they slipped out anyway, sounding strangled and pathetic.

Sam glanced across at her briefly before looking back at the road. "Bit late for that, isn't it? And where's home to you now anyway? I thought your house got destroyed?"

Marnie didn't answer, just scrunched down deeper in her seat. Damn him, he was right. There was no home for her to go back to. Her house was broken, her belongings covered in mud. Everything worth salvaging was stuffed in the bag on the back, getting sprayed in dust. She didn't want to look at Sam anymore. He was cute, but looking at him just reminded her of all that she'd lost.

• • • • • • •

Ordinarily, Sam enjoyed skidding around corners on gravel roads. But the squeak that had escaped Marnie's tightly clenched lips sent a flash of guilt through him. She was probably still traumatized from the earthquake and the hundreds of aftershocks since, poor girl. He wasn't being very sensitive to her, rally-driving along the country roads he knew like the back of his hand, but which were completely unfamiliar territory to her. But he was glad to wipe that disdainful sneer off her face all the same.

He had no idea what Aunty Magda was thinking, agreeing to take on a new hand without at least a brief interview first. Now the fallout of her hare-brained scheme was going to be left to him to deal with. The last thing he needed was a useless city girl with issues to deal with.

He pulled up a little way away from the house, outside the hay shed. Before he could say or do anything, she pulled her seat belt off and glared at him. "You drive like a dick head," she said bluntly. "If you did that in Christchurch you'd get pulled over so fast…"

"We're not in Christchurch," he said just as curtly.

It was just a plain statement of fact, but the flash of hurt and sadness in her eyes was obvious and in an instant he felt every inch the dick head she'd called him. She was biting her lip, obviously trying to keep from crying and he felt an impulse to try to comfort her. As annoying as she was, she was still a girl. He didn't like making girls cry; at least, not this way.

"Hey," he said, his voice softening as he reached for her. She pulled her arm away from him before he could touch her again, a near feral ferocity transforming her pretty face.

"You can go fuck yourself!"

She wrenched the door open and ran. He was stunned for a second, then he realized he was going to have to go after her. She didn't have a clue where she was or where she was headed. She was impressively fast in those stupid shoes though. At first he didn't hurry after her too quickly. He figured the electric fence would stop her when she got to it, but she put her hand on the post and jumped it as though she'd been hopping farm fences all her life.

"Hey! Stop! Girl…" What was her name again? He couldn't remember as he broke into a run after her. She was headed for the paddock with the bull in it, assuming she didn't break her ankle before she got to old Henry.

• • • • • • •

Marnie ran with tears in her eyes, blurring her vision. Everything was green here. Green and occasionally brown. She dodged the brown bits as she ran, not knowing where she was going, but knowing she didn't want to be anywhere near that man. He was the worst. She'd come all this way and now she was being dragged around and yelled at. It wasn't fair.

She could hear him shouting after her, but she ignored whatever it was he was saying. "Stop… Bull…"

"Bullshit," she growled to herself. "Swearing at me even now. Dick."

Just then she saw the mouth of a concrete tunnel. She bolted inside it, not really knowing why. As soon as she was inside it, she stopped, panting. It had been a while since she'd sprinted like that.

He must have been right on her ass, because within seconds he was there, crouching outside the mouth of her little hiding place. He fixed his eyes right on her and crooked a finger at her.

"Come here, little girl," he drawled.

Little girl. The words made her stomach do flip-flops. She didn't know why.

"I'm not going anywhere with you. I'll live here if I have to."

"You're in a ditch," he said. "It floods with farm runoff."

"Runoff?"

"Sheep shit."

"Oh, god! Gross! What the…" She came crawling out as fast as possible under his less than amused gaze. "Is there anything not covered in fucking filth out here?"

"Watch your mouth," he warned. "Aunty Magda doesn't like swearing, and neither do I."

"Oh, ick…" She was still too grossed out by the filth on her hands, especially considering its origin. She looked around for something to wipe her fingers on. There was nothing. Except—he was standing there, already covered in dust and dirt as far as she could see.

Following her impulse, Marnie reached out and wiped her hands on his shirt. The moment her fingers made contact with his torso, she realized that his body was hard underneath that fabric. Rock hard. She hadn't felt a body on a man like that since… well, since ever. For a second, she forgot that she hated him. She forgot everything, including the quakes and…

"What the hell!" He swatted her hands away, the flat of his palm making sharp contact with the back of hers. "Whaddya think you're doing?"

"Doesn't make any difference to you, does it," she smirked, satisfied that she'd gotten her own back. The two muddy handprints on his stomach looked good. Sort of…

intimate.

He cut his eyes at her, but she thought she saw a slight flicker at the corner of his lips too. He didn't really seem to care about the extra dirt, but he had an issue with her, that much was obvious.

"Little brat," he growled. "You're going to end up with your rear tanned if you don't watch out. Come on. Aunty Magda is going to want to know where you are."

He turned on his heel and started walking away, leaving her with her mouth open, her mind replaying those words over and over. Tanned rear? What was he threatening her with exactly? And why did it excite her so damn much?

Now that they were both walking, she had a hard time catching up with him. His legs were a lot longer than hers, and he was wearing far more practical footwear. Maybe she should get some boots. Not that there was anything even faintly resembling a store anywhere around here. Looking around, all she could see was grass, more grass, a few trees planted in heavy lines, and then the mountains in the distance. Animals dotted the rolling terrain, but that was about it. A sense of isolation started to sink into her bones and she hurried a little more so as not to be alone.

"Don't run off again," he said gruffly as she got within a few steps of him. "We've got a bull in that paddock over there and he'll go for you if he gets a chance."

"Ohhhhh, that's what you were saying," she said. "I thought you were swearing at me."

"I was," he said, turning to face her. She stopped hurriedly, almost running into him.

"You've got to start listening," he said, his hands on his hips as he looked down at her, the muscle in his jaw twitching. "You don't seem to know why you're here, and having known you for five minutes, I'm guessing that's because you didn't listen when you were told."

"You don't know me!"

"You're right. I don't. But I know you haven't taken a thing I've said on board since I started talking, and if you keep it up, I'll have to smack it into your little ass."

• • • • • • •

Sam hadn't meant to actually say that, but the threat slipped out before he could stop it. This girl was about the most spankable chick he'd ever met. From the second she'd opened her mouth, he'd wanted to lay his hand, or maybe his belt across her ass. She filled out her jeans nicely; he gave her credit for that.

She stared at him, shock written all over her face. He was ready for her to go off again, but to his surprise, she didn't. A red hue suffused her face and she pulled her eyes away from him and looked down at the grass.

"Shut up," she mumbled. "Dick."

Her swearing was undermined by the fact she couldn't even look at him. She sounded petulant and small, and really in need of that spanking he was talking about.

Maybe nobody had ever laid down the law for her before. It wouldn't have surprised him. He was curious about her, why she was out here. She obviously didn't like the country much, so if she'd had anywhere else to be, or anyone to be with, he reckoned she would have taken that option.

"That's enough of the back chat," he said, putting a deeper note in his voice, same as he did when the farm dogs were acting up.

She didn't answer back, just folded her arms over her chest defensively and looked out to the distance.

"Come on," he said. "Magda will have Milo and super wines. Maybe some bubble log, if you're lucky."

• • • • • • •

"What's bubble log?" She didn't really care, but she had to break the silence somehow as she followed him up the cracked concrete path to the house.

Sam raised an eyebrow as he looked back over his shoulder at her. "How can you not know what bubble log is? CWI ladies have been making it for generations! I thought it was a childhood staple."

Marnie shrugged. "I'm from the city, remember? We don't have the CWI there. The 'c' in it stands for 'country,' not 'city.' And city women have more to do with their time than join ladies' institutes and sit around talking about knitting and baking all day."

Biting her lip to fight back the giggles that threatened to erupt from her at the furious expression on Sam's face, she gave him an innocent smile.

"How do you know so much about the CWI then, being from the city and all?"

"I have a grandma. Well, actually, I *had* a grandma." She swallowed. "The earthquake claimed her."

"I'm sorry."

She bit her lip again, forcing back tears this time, rather than giggles, as memories floated back. Good memories of special times she'd shared with her grandma were overshadowed by the horrendous nightmare of the earthquake that had been so terrifying and claimed so many lives. She would not cry. Not here, not now. She'd shed enough tears over the past two weeks to last a lifetime.

"And Grandma *liked* baking, dammit!"

Sam's hand on her shoulder, the strong fingers gripping gently, comfortingly, tipped her over the edge. She tried to shrug him off as tears stung her eyes, wanting to preserve some dignity, but he ignored her silent protest. Instead, he drew her in toward him as she lost the battle against her tears and he held her against his hard body, one hand tangled in her hair, the other rubbing her back, as she cried into his shirt.

It felt good, being wrapped in his arms. His body was hard, strong, and muscular, and he was much taller than she realized, because her head nestled perfectly just under his throat. She felt safe, but more than a little embarrassed. She barely knew this man, yet she was snivelling all over his shirt. Still, he didn't seem to mind, and it was nice having him be kind to her instead of bossy.

She swiped at her eyes with the back of her hand, sheepish. "But I still don't know what bubble log is."

The wink Sam gave her made her insides somersault. "You'll find out soon enough."

Before they reached the veranda, the front door opened and a woman who appeared to be in her late sixties bustled out, her face lined, her eyes crinkled at the corners from her wide smile.

"Welcome! You must be Marnie. I'm Magda, Sam's aunt."

Marnie looked around. "Who is Sam?"

"Samuel!" Magda scolded. "Did you not introduce yourself? Where are your manners?"

"No, he didn't," Marnie said. "I was expecting someone called Sam, but that could have been a woman, for all I knew. He didn't tell me anything about himself at all!"

Although she'd enjoyed being in his arms just minutes before, now Marnie enjoyed the blush that crept across Sam's face. He squirmed slightly under his aunt's scrutinizing glare and it was all she could do not to giggle with glee. Certain she'd found an ally in his aunty Magda, she put on her most innocent smile.

"He was late to pick me up," she informed the older woman.

"By about two minutes, brat!" Sam growled. He flexed his hands, glaring at her menacingly.

"And he drove like a maniac on the way home, fishtailing around the corners," she snarked.

"Samuel!" Magda scolded again, the welcoming smile having completely left her face.

A tingle went down her spine as Sam glowered at her fiercely, his hands now clenched tightly into fists at his sides.

"And that was after he threw my bag onto the back of that dirty, dusty old ute!"

Magda sniffed and turned away. "There's a lot of dust and dirt out here, love," she murmured. "You'd best get used to it."

Marnie felt deflated as Magda's heavy footsteps echoed down the corridor inside. Looked like the older woman wasn't going to stick up for her after all, and she'd be left to deal with that ... that brute, alone. She didn't belong here at all, she was totally out of place.

"You tried to get me in trouble, brat!" Sam growled. "You probably would have, too, if you'd left off the bit about the dust. Aunty Magda is a stickler for manners. And for punctuality. But it hasn't rained for six weeks; dust is just a fact of life out here. None of us like it much, but we've all had to get used to it."

"Oh." She didn't know what else to say. Having experienced Sam's kindness, she felt the tiniest twinge of guilt at having tried to use his aunt to gang up on him.

"So what happens if I do get you in trouble?" Marnie couldn't resist asking.

"You get your ass smacked."

She snorted. "Yeah, whatever! By who?"

Sam glared at her. "Me."

"I'd like to see you try. Dick." It was a direct challenge, especially with the insult tacked on the end, but one she very much hoped Sam wouldn't take her up on. Not yet, anyway.

"You'll get that chance pretty soon, brat," he assured her.

Leaning his shoulder against the front of the house, Sam stood on one leg to rid himself of his filthy boots. Marnie knew she should do the same, but she couldn't bring to herself to drop the subject just yet. It was far too intriguing. Almost as intriguing as Sam's socks, which were stripy red, blue, green, and yellow with the individual toes each a different neon colour.

"So how does that even work, anyway? How do you not get in trouble when you screw up?"

Sam exhaled loudly, probably with the exertion of taking

off his boots, but possibly with frustration at her questions. "I'm the boss here, not Aunty Magda. So if I screw up, I have to fix it."

"And if I screw up?"

"You probably get your ass smacked."

"No, I don't think so. I'm an adult. You can't hit me." Although she spoke determinedly, she felt her face heating up under Sam's penetrating stare. He was towering above her, his legs hip-width apart, with his arms folded across his chest in a manly alpha-male way that made her feel small, helpless, and vulnerable. His whole stance told her that he could, indeed, hit her if he chose to. His whole stance told her that smacking her butt not only could be done, but it wouldn't take very much effort at all. She was small—a hair over five foot four in her strappy shoes—and he had to be well over six foot tall.

"Come on, take your shoes off. Magda will be waiting."

Bending down to unbuckle her expensive, strappy sandals, she felt Sam's disapproval wash over her.

"I hope you brought some more appropriate footwear," he said. "You won't last five minutes trying to work in those things."

"No, I didn't," she snapped, straightening to glare at him. "I didn't bring the right footwear. I didn't bring the right clothes. I didn't bring any fucking foam sticks or bubble wood or whatever it is. It's all wrong, so you may as well get it over with and tell me how wrong and terrible my whole existence is." She waved her arms in an encompassing manner.

He did not look amused by her outburst. "I'll deal with you when Magda goes out to tend the goats," he said, his tone grim.

"Yee haw," she said, mockingly, putting on an American accent for no reason other than she didn't really know how to take the piss out of the country lifestyle without it. "Grind some chickens and pick some cows."

He shook his head curtly, turned on his socked heel, and

walked inside.

She followed after him, feeling a little hollow in the pit of her stomach. This guy was big, and she was pissing him off, almost on purpose.

The moment she stepped into the farmhouse kitchen with Magda, she felt better. Magda was a calm, kindly presence and Sam didn't seem to be quite as scary when she was there. He obviously respected the older woman a lot, and she seemed fond of him too.

Bubble log turned out to be awesome, rice bubbles mixed with honey and sugary goodness to make a slice that was chewy and crunchy at the same time. She had two pieces and would have had a third if not for Sam's brow lifting a fraction and igniting her nerves.

"You help Marnie get settled in, Sam," Magda said once she was satisfied Marnie had been fed and watered. "I'm out to milk."

She bustled out of the room, leaving them alone together again.

"Come on," Sam said. "Your room's upstairs."

She followed him with no small amount of trepidation. The house was old enough to have been built just the slightest bit before people got tall. Sam had to stoop under some of the doorways, and he basically filled the narrow staircase leading upward. The room he took her to was small but clean with little flowers on the wallpaper and a crocheted blanket covering the double bed. The furniture was all from the early sixties, dated, but it would do.

"Not exactly city standards I'm sure, but…"

"It's fine," she interrupted him with a shrug.

"Good," he said. "Now, to pick up where we left off…"

She had no idea what he was talking about, but she felt his hands on her waist and the world spin and then she came down prone over his lap. He'd sat on the bed and pulled her down on top of him, his hard legs beneath her hips, one strong arm wrapped around her waist, snugging her tight to his body.

"Fuck! What! Hey!"

He'd been warning her practically since they met, but that didn't mean she was any less shocked—and it definitely didn't mean she was just going to let him do this to her. She fought against him with every bit of her strength, trying to break free of his grasp.

• • • • • • •

She was panicking, bucking over his thighs. Sam was experienced enough in dealing with spoiled, spirited fillies to know if he knew if he let her up, all he'd be teaching her to do was to act out when he spanked her—and he had a damn good idea that he'd be spanking her a lot, so she may as well get used to this position now.

"Settle down," he soothed.

"Let me up!"

"That's not going to happen," he said, keeping a firm hold on her as she twisted and squirmed.

"Sam, you let me up now or… or…"

She didn't have much to threaten him with and they both knew it. For better or worse, she was stuck out here with him—and he with her. Sam didn't intend to have some stroppy city chick giving him attitude for the next however long.

"Just let me up, okay?"

She sounded a lot smaller now. He could hear the breath catching in her throat. She was genuinely scared, probably because she didn't know what she was in for and probably because she knew she deserved whatever it was.

"I'll let you up when I'm done with you," he said, patting her butt.

His touch set off another set of squirms and bucks, much as he'd expected it would. Handling a spoiled girl wasn't all that different from handling horses. Had to be calm and patient and above all, firm. Make doing the right thing easy, and make sure that they knew misbehaviour wasn't going to work.

Horses tended to learn quite a lot quicker than humans though. As he held Marnie in place and let her go through her struggles, he was thinking about how he was going to introduce her to the horses. He'd have to start with one of the older, calmer geldings first. Taxi, probably. You could put anyone on Taxi and he'd plod around the trek and return to base pretty much on autopilot. But really, he couldn't wait for this girl to meet Trixie, the pint-sized pinto with an attitude. That little mare could be as much of a brat as Marnie was shaping up to be. They'd either love each other or hate each other.

As she settled down over his lap again, he gave her another gentle pat and held on as she flipped out, but less intensely and for not quite as long as she had the previous couple of times.

"Good girl," he murmured as she started to settle with his palm steady on her bottom.

• • • • • • •

There was something in his voice, a soothing quality that made the deeper part of her relax. When he'd pulled her over his lap, she'd been anticipating blinding pain and god knows what else, but he'd barely touched her so far, and his big palm spread across her butt didn't exactly feel bad.

"Please don't spank me..." Marnie could barely believe she was begging him like this. "I'm... uhm... sorry?" She tried the word, not really liking how it felt in her mouth.

"You're not sorry yet," he said. "You don't have any reason to be. This is about giving you one."

"No!" she said quickly. "I am sorry, seriously, I am. Really."

"Uh huh." He didn't sound convinced. "What are you sorry for?"

"Uhhhmm... I'm sorry you don't like my shoes."

His palm left her butt and returned with a swift smack.

"Owwww!" she screamed as his hand met her bottom, not because it hurt too bad, but because she was expecting it to.

"You can cut the drama," he said with a snort. "When you get spanked properly, you can make sounds like that, but not for this one. This is a warning. If you act out like you've been doing since you got here, giving me attitude and mouthing off, you're going to get spanked. Hard. I need someone out here to help me, and by the sounds of things you've got a lot to learn. I don't have time to argue with you all day."

With that, his palm landed on the seat of her shorts with another crisp swat. It didn't hurt, but it also didn't not hurt. To her surprise, what it mostly did was send a hot blush through her body, making her face burn more than her bottom did.

He repeated the treatment a dozen or so more times, working his palm over her bottom with those slaps that made her blush and squirm. She was being spanked. Actually spanked. She couldn't believe it, even though it was currently happening. Every time his palm landed against her butt, it sent a thrill through her body and made her hips dance. She tried to stay still, but she couldn't help it. It was doing things to her.

After twelve or so smacks, he seemed to be satisfied that she'd learned whatever lesson it was he'd been teaching. Marnie was just squeezing her thighs together, trying not to give her secret away. She hadn't been with a guy in a long time and being pressed up against this big beast of a man, his hands so close to all the most intimate areas of her body, it was making her react in a way that was anything but sorry.

"Do we have an understanding?"

"Yessir," she said quickly, the 'sir' part coming from some random part of her brain.

"Good girl. You know, you can be cute when you're not being a brat," he said, rubbing her stinging butt gently.

She bit her lower lip and tried to not make the noises she

was tempted to make. Not cries of pain, but sounds of something else. Thankfully her shorts were covering all the strategic parts of her anatomy, so he couldn't know that while he'd been spanking her, she'd been getting wet.

After a couple more minutes, he let her up. She was both glad to be allowed to stand, and a little disappointed it was all over. Keeping her face turned away from him, she studiously avoided his gaze in case he saw the truth of her reaction written there.

He stood up, smoothing his palms over his jeans. "Look at me, Marnie."

She couldn't, not until he took her by the arm and used the fingers of his other hand to tip her chin up.

"I know you've been through a hell of a time," he said, looking down into her blushing face. "And I know this place is about as far away from home as you can get—and maybe that's a good thing."

"It's not a good thing," she insisted. "Why is it a good thing? Do you like seeing me floundering in a place I don't fit, like a fish out of water?"

Sam chuckled, and she wanted to punch him. He'd already made her butt burn and now he was laughing at her misfortune? He really was a piece of work.

The glare she gave him was one she'd perfected over the years, designed to make even the most intimidating of people quiver. But Sam didn't flinch. Instead he smiled, his eyes crinkling up at the corners in a way that made her want to melt, but she steeled her resolve. She was not going to succumb to his charms. Not after the way he'd just manhandled her over his lap and… and… she couldn't even think about that right now. Not when her butt was still tingling and her pussy was still wet

"It's a fresh start," he said simply, interrupting her thoughts.

"Maybe I don't want a fresh start?" she snapped. "Maybe I want my old life back?"

"Maybe you do," Sam conceded. "But that's not likely to

happen, is it? The earthquake changed everything."

Although she continued to glare at Sam, and even stomped her foot for good measure, he still didn't react. If anything, his smile widened, like perhaps he found her amusing. She huffed dejectedly and pouted.

"Come on, let's go find you some decent boots and I'll show you around."

"I don't want to be shown around." She knew she sounded petulant and spoiled, but she didn't care. She didn't care about anything anymore.

"Would you rather another spanking? A proper one this time?" Gruff, growly Sam was back; his patience was obviously wearing thin.

A shiver went down Marnie's spine at his tone, as she considered his words. What was a *proper* spanking? Had the one he'd just given her been improper? She giggled. Yes, *improper* probably was the right word to describe what Sam had just done to her. She'd quite liked it, though. And because she'd liked the improper spanking so much, she assumed that a proper one wouldn't be nearly so enjoyable. Life seemed to be like that: the proper things were never as much fun.

She couldn't help asking the question anyway, though. "What does a *proper* spanking entail? How is it different to what you just did?"

Judging by the way Sam's hands clenched and unclenched by his sides and the way his jaw stiffened, he didn't like her question much. But then, that didn't really surprise her. So far, Sam didn't seem to like very much about her at all.

"It will be hard, and it will hurt," he growled. He flexed his right hand. "Shall I show you?"

She gulped, unsure why she was still intentionally pissing him off, and shook her head. "Nah, I'm good. I guess you can show me around."

Sam walked to the window and heaved it upward, sliding the bolt into a hole halfway up the frame to hold it in place.

A blast of hot air rushed inward, hitting Marnie in the face.

"We can start here if you like." Sam pointed out the window. "See those mountains? We do overnight treks out there. And follow that river along, that's mostly where we go on the shorter treks. Four hours return to the waterfall." His voice was animated as he described the land he quite obviously loved.

Marnie took a step closer so she could see where Sam was indicating. As she stepped forward, he moved back slightly and she ended up wedged between his body and the window frame, her shoulder up against the hard ridges of his muscular arm. Her traitorous body remembered being held by that strong arm just moments before and reacted; her shoulder burned at his touch, sparks shot to her core. She couldn't see the river. She couldn't even see the mountains. All she could focus on was Sam, and the way his touch made her feel.

Sam continued to speak but Marnie was oblivious to his words. She felt heat rise to her face as she remembered the way it had felt as he'd held her fast, upended over his dusty thighs, his huge palm resting lightly on her rear. She was so confused! The man next to her was a brute. One minute she was in his arms while he comforted her, the next he was whaling away on her ass. Even worse, she'd enjoyed both situations.

She realized, too late, that Sam had stopped speaking and was looking at her expectantly, as if waiting for her to answer a question.

"Do you?" The slight quirk of his brow sent her insides flip-flopping madly again.

"Huh?"

"Socks." Sam sighed loudly, exasperated. "Did you listen to anything that I said?"

"We-ell..." Marnie drew the word out into several syllables. "I did at first," *and then I just started thinking about you, instead of listening.*

"Do you have any socks?"

Marnie thought. She did, of course, in her bag. But where was her bag? Was it still on the back of that filthy ute? Crap!

She nodded.

"Good. Get them. We're going for a walk." Sam gripped her upper arm tightly and held her close, just inches from his face. "And you listen to me, girl. You're not to go running off again, understand? This is a farm. There's dangers here you know nothing about. This isn't the city, you know. So you stick with me, all right?"

"Yessir," she whispered, hardly daring to breathe.

• • • • • • •

Leading the way down the stairs, Sam tried to rein in his anger, but he only partially succeeded. What the hell had Aunty Magda been thinking? She hadn't—that much was obvious. The new girl was so far out of place he couldn't have found anyone less suitable if he'd tried. She was disobedient, far too sassy, spoiled, and didn't listen when she was being spoken to. None of which boded well for her future at Terako Treks.

"Get your bag," he snapped at her as they got close to the front door. "Grab your socks out of it and leave it all here; I don't have time to wait for you to fluff about."

She wasn't moving. He turned to glare at her and found her standing, staring at him, with her arms folded across her chest in an outrageous display of defiance.

"A gentleman would get it for me," she said accusingly. "Not very good service here, is it?"

"We've been through this already, brat," he growled. "You're here to work, not be serviced, and I'm not a gentleman. I've never claimed to be one, and I won't be starting now. I'm not going to run around after you doing things for you that you're perfectly capable of doing for yourself. Besides which, you're not exactly a lady. Not with the mouth on you that you've got."

"Bastard." She mumbled the word as she pushed past him and stomped down the rickety steps to the ute, her city shoes sending up clouds of dust.

"Watch your mouth," he warned. But he felt like a bastard as he watched her struggle to drag her big bag over the high sides of the ute and up the steps to the house.

Her body was rigid with tension as she pulled on her socks and she didn't say a word to him as he put several pairs of boots of varying sizes in front of her, spares they kept for riding guests who didn't bring their own.

"These are riding boots," he explained as she pulled the first pair on. "We'll have to get you some proper work boots, but these will do in the meantime. They'll be better than those strappy sandals, anyway. Do they fit okay?"

She glared in response, so he took that to be a 'yes.'

As she followed him out to the barn he wasn't sure which was worse: her sassy, bad-mannered attitude she'd been displaying or the stony silence she was giving him now.

Throwing open the big double doors of the barn, he breathed in deeply of the familiar horsey scent.

"God, it stinks in here!" Marnie's voice sounded nasally and distorted and when he turned to face her, she was pinching her nostrils shut between her finger and thumb. He stifled a laugh. This smell was nothing. When it was full with horses on a hot day… that was when it really stunk.

"Do you know how to muck out stalls?"

Her blank expression told him all he needed to know.

"It's when you clean out all the soiled and wet sawdust," he explained. He grabbed one of the rakes hanging up on the wall. "You use this."

"You want me to… to… shovel shit?"

"Not right now, no. But this will be one of your jobs, when it needs to be done."

"You can't make me touch shit," she moaned, her desperate tone barely above a whisper. "Nobody told me about this."

She looked pale, like the very thought of mucking out a

stall terrified her and he almost felt sorry for her. Until he remembered why she probably didn't know anything about her current situation.

"You mean, you weren't listening when you were told about this," he corrected.

"No," she insisted. "Nobody told me."

• • • • • • •

He was looking at her that way again, his brow drawing down over his eyes. She had disappointed him. She felt like the shit he wanted her to shovel. Like something lower than whatever dung was undoubtedly on his boot. This guy was hot and capable and he was probably already with some country girl who knew all about horses and had the right shoes and who didn't make him scowl every six seconds for some new infraction.

The sensation of arousal from that spanking he'd given her had long faded with the smell of manure. Instead the feelings of inadequacy, disgust, and rejection triggered her flight impulse.

"Okay, that's it. I'm going home. Seriously. Take me back to the bus stop. I'll just wait there until one comes."

She felt sick to her stomach with longing for something familiar. It was bad enough when she'd had to deal with everything being covered in dust. But now he was expecting her to clean up after horses? That was about as far beneath her as any job could be. She shouldn't be surprised though. He'd treated her with pretty obvious disdain since she got there. Maybe he thought she was too dumb to notice the way his lip curled, or how his eyes darkened every time she didn't know some stupid farm thing.

"I can't take this," she said, backing away, holding her hands up in surrender. "This was a huge mistake. You know it. I know it. Let's just cut our losses."

He leaned against a stable door and looked at her with an expression even worse than derision: pity.

"Where are you going to go, little girl?"

The words *little girl* made her squirm inside, but she was too upset to give way to that feeling. She was close to crying again, but she wasn't going to. Not this time.

"I don't care," she said, backing out of the stable. "Anywhere but here."

He watched her, not moving. The muscle in his jaw ticked, but he didn't say anything. He just watched her as she got further and further away. She didn't stop until her boots hit grass, then she stalled, knowing there was probably a fence behind her.

"Come on," she said. "You can get rid of me right now. I know you want to."

"You don't know what I want," he said, rubbing his hands together in a gesture that made her seat tingle. "But let me tell you what I'd like right now. That's for you to stop talking about leaving, and start learning. Mucking out is just one part of this job. It's probably the worst, but there's other things that make up for it."

"Like what?"

"Like the horses."

Just as he said those words, she felt a puff of warm air against the back of her neck.

She turned her head to find herself looking into the long face of a horse that must have ambled across the paddock to inspect her. It was gold- and white-coloured, marked sort of like a cow, and had a white stripe running down over its head. Surprisingly soft, but very strong lips took a nibble at her hair.

"Hey!" She frowned. "What are you doing?"

The horse made a sound like it was laughing at her and lifted its head up high, waving it back and forth.

"That's Trixie," Sam said with a grin. "She's young and pretty green still, but she's a character."

"She's a terrible hairdresser," Marnie grumbled, smoothing her hair back from her face. "Am I going to have

31

to ride this horse out of here, or are you going to take me back to the bus stop?"

Sam's face fell into a more serious demeanour again. "First things first, you are not to try to ride Trixie. She's broken, but…"

"She's broken?" Marnie frowned. "That's so sad. What happened?"

"I mean," Sam smiled and paused, as if he was trying not to bust out laughing as he walked over to her. "I mean she's been trained to accept a bridle and a saddle and a rider, but she still acts out a lot because she's only four years old. It'll take her a few more years to settle down and be a safe ride for someone like you."

"Someone like me. You mean someone too dumb for anything better than shovelling shit. Let's go already."

"Marnie," he said, his use of her name making her quiver. "You're not going anywhere. I need a hand, and you need a place to stay. We're just going to have to make this work."

"Why can't you find some other help? I'm pretty much the worst option you could get."

"Well, maybe," he agreed gallingly. "But I'm not having you run off into the countryside."

"So I'm, what, a prisoner here? You're going to stop me from leaving if I want to?" She lifted her chin in challenge, and found him meeting her rebellious gaze with a steady, stern look.

"That's right, little girl."

• • • • • • •

The stunned look on her face told Sam she hadn't been expecting that answer. Truthfully, he hadn't thought about it before he gave it. He meant it, though. She was spoiled, and she was a brat. She was going to take a lot of teaching to be useful. She was a problem—but she was his problem and he had no intention of letting her run out on him. Or, more precisely, running her off. Her inexperience wasn't her fault, and he hadn't exactly rolled out the welcome mat.

"You can't keep me here," she said, her outrage somewhat blunted as Trixie nuzzled her again, trying to take hold of the strap of her tank top. "Cut that out, horse!"

"You have somewhere else to stay? You have money for accommodation lined up?"

Her face told him that the answer to both questions was a resounding no.

"You're going to pay me?"

"The law is pretty clear on having to pay workers," he said, rubbing the scruff on his chin. "Even totally inexperienced ones."

"Well, I haven't seen an employment contract."

"True. Aunty Magda probably didn't want to welcome you with paperwork. I'll get that sorted. You'll start on $16.50 an hour and…"

"Minimum wage," she sneered.

"You get room and board too, brat. It's not a bad deal for an apprenticeship."

He watched as she thought about that. Trixie helped by nuzzling her ear.

"Stop it, horsie!" She giggled, nudging Trixie's head away again.

She was more than cute when she smiled. She was utterly adorable. Her sparkling green eyes, which could hold such derision, lit up with real joy. Her blonde hair, which looked to have been carefully straightened, was starting to curl where Trixie had mouthed it, and the dust she hated was all over her shorts and her top. The length of bare leg between her shorts and the top of her riding boots was alluringly curvy. Sam felt a bolt of attraction as she wriggled next to the horse, who had taken a relentless interest in her.

"I can't wait to see the part where you outline your unorthodox disciplinary policies," she grinned, half-turning to rub Trixie's nose with her fingers.

The position made that shorts-covered rear stick out,

causing more than one part of him to twitch with interest. *Don't screw the crew, Sam*, he reminded himself silently. Besides, she was almost ten years younger than him, and obviously emotionally unsteady from the quakes. He had to get his impulses under control and take care of her, both as a new employee and as a guest of the family.

"Okay," she said as Trixie continued to nuzzle her. "I guess I can stay. But I'm not shovelling…"

"You're going to learn to muck out, and clean tack, and saddle a horse. You're going to learn to pick hooves and wash down and when you've learned all that, you'll learn to ride."

"You're going to teach me all that?"

"Mhm."

"That's a lot," she said doubtfully.

"You're a smart girl, you'll get the hang of it."

She didn't look convinced, but as she softly petted Trixie's nose, she seemed to come around.

"One condition."

"What's that?" He thoroughly expected her to say that he couldn't spank her.

"You can't growl at me for not knowing things I have no way of knowing, or act like I'm some piece of shit because I didn't come with a whole bag of horse costumes or whatever it is you people wear."

"Fair enough," he agreed with a laugh. "I'll take you down to Farmlands tomorrow and we'll get you sorted."

"Okay," she said. "Deal."

He extended his hand and she slipped her smaller one into his. He gave her a firm shake.

"So you are my boss," she said as their hands separated.

"Uh huh."

"Haven't really had a boss before," she said thoughtfully. "I've always been freelance. This is going to be so weird."

"In a lot of ways," he agreed. "We start work at six."

"Six! I don't get up before, like, ten. Nine at the earliest."

"I'll get you up at half past five," he said. "When we get

busy, the horses need to be fed and ready, we have to make sure they're still sound, have to make sure…"

"I don't get up that early though," she said stubbornly, as if it was up for negotiation.

"You will here."

"Uhm, I won't though."

"Little girl, I will drag you out of bed, spank your ass, and send you down to breakfast every morning if I have to," he threatened, the growl back in his voice.

• • • • • •

Marnie scowled. Five-thirty? Seriously? That was still night-time! No way was she getting out of bed at that hour, it just wasn't happening. But the way Sam was standing there staring at her, all stern and everything, she knew that she probably wouldn't have too much choice. He'd already shown her how much stronger than her he was, so she knew he wouldn't have any difficulty physically dragging her out of bed if he chose to.

She pouted. "I suppose I can try. But I'll be grumpy," she warned. "Very grumpy. I don't do mornings."

"I can fix grumpy." Sam grinned.

"And I'll need coffee," she said. "Lots of coffee."

"You can have all the coffee you want."

"Mornings hate me," she declared. "You're going to regret this."

"Mmm, probably," Sam agreed. "But we'll just have to make the best of it, won't we?"

Trixie blew down the back of her neck, making her jump. She'd forgotten about the horse standing directly behind her. Turning, she stroked the velvety muzzle. Marnie had never been this close to a horse before, but with the fence between them, she felt safe enough. What was it Sam had said she'd be doing? Putting on saddles and something to do with hooves? That sounded a bit scarier. She sure wished she'd been listening when her aunt had told her about this job.

"So how many horses are on this place anyway?" she asked, stepping back from Trixie. "And where is that river you showed me out the window? Are there any fish in it?"

Sam grinned. He was so handsome when he did that; the way his eyes lit up made her wish she actually fit in at a place like this and that he could see her as more than a burden.

"There's trout in the river," he told her. "And we have a couple of dozen horses, not all of them are in work. How many we have here at the barn depends on how busy we are."

Marnie gulped. She was going to have to learn the names of two dozen horses? Sam must have noticed the dumbfounded expression on her face because he chuckled, and his eyes crinkled up at the corners as his rumbly laughter washed over her, making her insides turn to molten lava. Damn the man for having such an effect on her!

"Come on, little girl, let's go see the river. You been on a farm bike before?" He held a hand out to her in invitation but she ignored it.

There were those words again. Her tummy clenched.

"Why do you keep calling me that?" she demanded. "I'm not a child."

"No," he agreed, "you're not. But still, it fits." He stretched his hand out further toward her and wrapped her fingers in his, tugging gently. "I want to show you the rest of the herd, and the waterfall."

Sparks shot through her palm as their hands connected and her whole body prickled with a kind of energy that she couldn't describe. Was Sam feeling it too?

With her fingers locked in his, Marnie had no choice but to follow along behind Sam. She had to scurry to keep up with his long strides and the borrowed boots, which were ever so slightly too small, rubbed against her heel with every step she took.

Sam led her around the other side of the barn to where a mud-encrusted two-wheeler motorbike was leaning against the wall. Like the ute he had picked her up in, it looked like it had seen better days.

"Come on, we'll take the bike."

Marnie froze. "You expect me to ride on that thing?"

Sam looked at her. "Sure! Why not?"

"It's filthy, for one thing." Marnie screwed up her nose. "What is even on it? It stinks!"

Shaking his head, Sam sighed. For someone who insisted he would teach her everything she would need to know to work here, he sure didn't have a lot of patience.

"It's a farm bike," Sam explained, speaking slowly, like he thought she was a bit daft. "Of course it's going to be dirty. But it's perfectly safe. And it beats walking. Come on!"

Marnie crossed her arms across her chest. "Nuh-uh. Can't make me."

"Oh, for fuck's sake," Sam growled, clenching his fists tightly by his sides. Somehow, his stern features looked even more handsome when his face was creased up into a frown.

"Aunty Magda doesn't like swearing," Marnie pointed out. "Isn't that what you said? If I'm not allowed to use naughty words, neither are you." She stabbed her finger in his general direction triumphantly, but her smile faded when Sam exhaled loudly and flexed his hands menacingly.

"If you don't want your ass smacked again, I suggest you be quiet and do as you're told," he snarled.

Pulling the bike upright and kicking the stand back up, Sam wheeled the bike around in a circle so it was facing the right way, then he threw his leg over the seat, balancing the machine between his dusty thighs. Marnie felt her face flush at the memory of lying across those very thighs not so long ago.

He held his hand out to her. "Get on," he ordered.

"Shouldn't we have helmets or something?"

Kicking the stand back down with his boot, Sam sighed. Then he gently leaned the bike over until the stand took its weight, then dismounted. "Yes, you're right, we probably should." He indicated back the way they'd just come. "Back into the barn."

Dragging her feet, Marnie followed Sam back into the barn. The smell of horses wasn't so overpowering this time, and her nose didn't wrinkle up in distaste of its own accord like it had the first time she'd entered the building. He turned left into a small room and turned on a light; as her eyes adjusted to the brightness after the dimness of the barn, Sam's bulk made him look like a giant.

She looked around. It was crammed full of horse paraphernalia—saddles, halter, bridles, reins, stirrups, and other things she didn't recognize. She had no idea what most of the stuff was for. Curious, she turned in a circle, staring at all the equipment. So many saddles! And she would have to clean them. Isn't that what he'd said?

"Lots of things in here for keeping disobedient little girls in line." There was a distinctly amused note in Sam's voice, and she quivered, her curious gaze finding a row of stirrup leathers hanging on a hook.

Keep her in line? Surely he didn't mean...

Pushed back against the wall, almost touching her boot, a selection of riding crops sat in a tall plastic bin. Her buttocks clenched involuntarily as Sam pulled one out and waved it at her before tapping it against his palm. She felt her eyes widen. *Surely not... No way was he smacking her with a riding crop!* She backed up a step, getting ready to run. This was too much.

Obviously sensing her trepidation, Sam reached past her and returned the riding crop to the bin. "Don't worry, little girl." His deep voice washed over her, soothing her. "As long as you do as you're told, you don't have anything to worry about."

Her heart pounded so loudly she was surprised Sam couldn't hear it. Emotions she didn't recognize had raced through her when he'd waved the crop at her like that, and now that he'd put it back where it belonged, she felt oddly disappointed. What would it feel like to have the crop biting into the tender flesh on her ass? Would it be exquisite, as his palm had been? Would the dampness return to her pussy, bringing her to a state of perfect, embarrassing arousal as the first spanking had done?

She could vaguely hear him talking in the background, but she was too busy thinking about the riding crop, and wondering how on earth she was going to get her head around all this stuff, to listen to him.

Crack! A sound like a gunshot exploded right beside her and she jumped, startled. She spun around, her hand on her chest in fright, her heart pounding even more.

Sam grinned, then reeled in his stock whip. "I thought that might get your attention," he chuckled. "You weren't listening to one word that I said, were you?"

The blank look she gave him clearly told him all he needed to know. Raising his arm, he cracked the whip again, whipping up the dirt in front of her feet, just about scaring the living daylights out of her. She put her hands up to her mouth to try to stifle her scream, and squeaked pathetically. She felt the colour drain from her face.

"What the actual fuck?" It came out as barely more than a whisper, but Sam heard. His face darkened as he raised one eyebrow.

"You might want to pay more attention, little girl," he growled, winding up his whip again. "Unless you want to find this whip cracking across your ass instead of next to it."

She squirmed under his penetrating stare. He had a way of making her feel so small, so naughty, with just a look and a stern word.

"As I was saying, when you weren't listening, helmets are compulsory here, for all riders. So you may as well find one that you like, and keep it; you're going to need it, eventually." He pointed the handle of his whip at the shelf in front of them. "Helmet. Find one that fits. Small on the left, bigger on the right."

"Do I get one of those too?" She asked the question as she pulled out various helmets. Most of them were black, but there were a couple of coloured ones too. There was a pink one, toward the smaller side, but not all the way down at the end. She pulled it on and put it on her head. It fit perfectly.

"A whip?" He grinned as he stepped forward and helped her adjust the buckle under the chin. "Oh, you'll get that alright."

It was obvious from his tone that he wasn't intending on giving her one of her own, rather he was talking about using it on her, teasing her with more bold innuendo.

"Mhm. Cute," he nodded, palming the helmet and rocking it back and forth, then side to side. "Very good. Suits you, little girl."

"How would you like it if I called you a little boy?" She frowned under the thick brim of the helmet.

"You can try," he smirked. "See what that gets you."

He was still holding that whip in his hand, coiled like a snake and probably just as dangerous. She thought about forming the words. She thought real hard, but they didn't come. There was nothing little about him, that was the thing. He was very... Big. In every way.

• • • • • • •

Did she have any idea how bloody adorable she looked, standing there pouting with her pink helmet, wrestling with herself to try to taunt him? God. Sam's heart swelled just looking at her. As much as she made him want to whip her ass every other minute, she also made him want to wrap her up and cuddle her and look after her. She needed looking after. She needed rules and discipline. She needed him to strip her and fuck her senseless...

Sam brought himself to reality with a start. Now he was standing there zoning out. Whatever she had was catching.

"Right," he said. "Good. Helmet. We can get going."

"What about your helmet?"

He never wore a helmet when he was riding the farm bike, or when he was riding the horses for that matter, unless there was a real reason to.

"I'll be alright," he said. "Just as long as you're protected."

"You're supposed to wear a helmet."

She was right. Legally everyone was supposed to wear them. He had one, somewhere. Not a riding helmet like she was wearing, but a bike one. Was it in his office?

"Hold on," he said. "Let me get it."

He had an office in the back of the stable where he did the books and signed riders in for treks and things. It needed a clean and a tidy up. He was sure he'd last seen that helmet here. Now where was it…

Five minutes or so later, the helmet eventually turned up beneath a pile of horse rugs.

Marnie looked at him with a disapproving stare as he chased a couple of spiders out of it and settled it over his head, visor up.

"Happy?" His voice was muffled a little by the chin protector.

"Delirious," she said sarcastically.

His hand was on the whip, twisting it free and sending the length of it out toward her with a flick of his wrist. The lash snaked through the air and found her butt in a heartbeat.

She yelped and jumped, clutching at the affected cheek. The whip had caught her just under those all too short shorts and he could see the pink little mark it had left in its wake.

"Jesus! Stop that!"

He smiled to himself. He could probably work the lash down into her cleavage and have that top off if he wanted. Instead he cracked the whip again, next to her feet this time. She jumped and danced on the spot, yelping even though he hadn't touched her.

"Stop it! That's not nice!"

"It's very nice," he purred. When she jumped, the sweet curves of her body moved in just the right way. She was a hot little thing and the longer he spent standing in front of her with a whip in his hand, the more he wanted to ply it across her body. He'd been whip-cracking for years, as a hobby and for the odd competition. It came in handy with stock sometimes too, but it had never been as much fun as it was right now.

She looked like she was about to get upset though, and toying with her wasn't fair. He had to get his act together and be the boss she needed him to be.

"Come on," he said, looping the whip back up and clipping it to his belt. "Let's go."

Marnie followed him back out to the bike. He got on it first and gestured behind him. "Climb on up."

CHAPTER THREE

She was nervous. Not just about going on a motorbike, which was new to her, but about being so close to Sam. Trying to do as she was told for once, Marnie slipped onto the back of the bike and sat there kind of awkwardly, just barely perched on the seat.

"Snug up," he said, taking the helmet off to talk to her. "Closer."

She blushed as she pushed up behind him, her breasts pressing against his back, spread legs making her sex push against the seam of her shorts, and then him too. This was damn near indecent. His powerful, but lean waist and hips meant that it was easy for her to practically wrap herself around him.

"Tighter," he said, taking hold of her hands. He pulled them around his waist, drawing her hard against him. God. She was practically humping him now. She could smell his scent, deep and earthy and masculine and...

The bike purred into life, vibration shot through her and she knew in an instant she was in trouble. Even before they set off she could feel her clit grinding against the seam of her shorts, the rumbling stimulating her completely indecently. There wasn't a bit of daylight between them as

43

they set off across the gorgeous green fields.

She couldn't focus on the scenery at all. All she could concentrate on were the sensations. He'd used his whip on her and the little zip of pain had made her feel a lot like the spanking had—hot and wet. Now she was grinding against his hard back, her breath coming in little gasps as they bumped over a gravel track.

Marnie tried everything she could not to come. She really did, but it was a physical thing she couldn't help. Every little bump and ridge took her that little bit closer, the steady vibration of the motor ramping her excitement up as she clung to him.

Her body was singing with sensation, her every experience with him up until that point feeding into her arousal. He'd lectured her, spanked her, whipped her, cuddled her when she cried, and now she was arching against him, her helmet pressing between his shoulder blades as her shamefully desperate loins ground on his back.

She came with a muffled cry, biting her lower lip as her hips rocked back and forth, rubbing her wet clit against her jeans. She was soaked between her thighs, totally in heat. Sam's muscled back flexing as he moved with the bike making her wet slit soak her panties as her orgasm rushed through her, every muscle tightening with the force of it.

Jesus. Christ. She couldn't believe it. She bit her lower lip as her pussy continued to quiver with orgasmic aftershocks that didn't abate until the bike slowed and then stopped a minute or two later.

Marnie was still trembling when he cut the engine off and stood up, removing the helmet to look at her. She couldn't meet his gaze.

"You alright?"

"Uhm hmm… uh huh." She tried to sound casual while blushing furiously.

"Scared of bikes?"

"Nope." She tried to jump off quickly, to close her legs so he wouldn't see the wet spot between her thighs, but instead of a nimble exit, she more or less tumbled off the bike and onto the grass.

Rushing around with a short curse, Sam helped her up, his strong arms wrapped around her as he stood her up on her feet. "You wouldn't be lying to me, would you, little girl?" He kept his arms around her as he looked down at her, as if he didn't want to let her get away too quickly.

Marnie stifled a guilty little embarrassed grin. If he had any idea what she'd just been doing against his back, he wouldn't be calling her little girl. He'd be... she didn't know what he'd do.

Although she didn't want to, she leaned against Sam, grateful for his strength. Her legs were like jelly and with trying to clamp her thighs tightly shut to hide her disgrace and the way her pussy was throbbing, she couldn't even stand. Her heart raced and her breath came in short, ragged little gasps that she tried to control, but as Sam continued to hold onto her she got the sense that he could see right through her. She could just about feel his brow rising as he figured out what she'd done, what she still wanted to do.

Her whole body tingled from the aftereffects of her orgasm. Sam's strong hands tightened around her, pulling her in closer against his hard body, making those tingles intensify, rippling down her spine. She wanted him so badly. Twisting her body slightly, she shoved her pelvis up against his thigh, the seam of his jeans catching against the front of her shorts and pressing against her clit, just about sending her into orbit. Sam shifted his leg slightly and it was all she could do to swallow her moan of pleasure.

A low groan sounded deep in her throat when Sam caught a handful of her hair and tugged it, yanking her head back, forcing her to look up at him. She couldn't look at him, not when she knew her eyes were still blazing with passion and her face was still red. But nor could she avoid his gaze; he held her head still and stared down at her, and it was then that she realized for certain that *he knew*. She blinked, wishing the ground would open up and swallow her whole. Sam smiled. It wasn't a friendly, kind smile meant to put her at ease but a smug, knowing one. A smile that turned her roiling insides upside down and inside out. A smile that told her he knew what she'd done. And he liked it. And he wasn't averse to helping her do it again.

She couldn't breathe, the air was too thick. And she couldn't move. It wasn't just Sam's hands holding her in place that rendered her immobile but the electricity that zinged through her entire body, pulsing and throbbing, making her muscles elastic, her body helpless under his touch. She froze.

"You're horny, aren't you, little girl?" It was more of a statement than a question, spoken in a voice husky with arousal.

"Yessir," she whispered. Every nerve ending was on fire. If she didn't get some relief soon, she'd self-combust.

Arching her back shifted her body forward and her stomach pressed against his crotch, his impressive erection stabbing into her abdomen. Smiling mischievously, she rubbed herself against him, blatantly coming onto him. She'd never had an orgasm twice in a row before, but she'd also never wanted a man as badly as she wanted Sam right then.

· · · · · · ·

Sam tightened his fist around Marnie's hair. The little minx! It was obvious she was hot for him. She was blushing and trying to avoid his gaze, for starters. But once he held her face still and fixed his eyes on hers, the passion shining brightly in their liquid depths was a clear giveaway. Not to mention the fact that he could feel her trembling, he could hear her quick, panting breaths, and he could smell it. The aroma of her drenched sex was unmistakeable and when he prised her thighs apart with his own, he could see her juices wetting the front of her shorts. He'd felt her squirming around on the back of the bike and wondered what she was doing; now he knew.

Looking down at her flared nostrils, her parted lips, the bold defiance in her eyes, made him hard. She was embarrassed, but she was also blatantly provocative. Her *come on, big boy!* signals were very clear. His swollen cock threatened to tear his pants apart at the seams. Mischief danced in her eyes a split second before she placed her hand against his crotch, cupping his balls through the fabric, sliding her hand back between his thighs, squeezing.

He swallowed.

"Fuck me." The words were precise, clipped and clear, but whispered.

Sam didn't need any further invitation. In one swift move he let go of her hair, spun her around and pushed her over the back of the motorbike, slapping her ass hard as she straddled the machine, one leg on either side of the wheel.

"This is what happens to naughty little girls who make themselves come," he growled, slapping her ferociously again, much harder than he'd done when he'd spanked her earlier. "They get smacked and fucked. Hard."

"Yessir."

"Is this what you want, little girl? To be fucked?"

She was beautiful, bent over the back of the bike, the tops of her thighs splotched pink from where he'd slapped her. He could feel her trembling under his hand. Or maybe it was his own trembling that he could feel; it was a while since a woman had come even close to having this effect on him.

"Yessir!" Desperation tinged her words. "Please!"

Reaching underneath her, he fumbled with the fastenings at her waist, silently cursing his clumsy fingers. Finally he undid the button and pulled down the zip, yanking her shorts down over her hips, dragging them and her underwear down her thighs roughly, exposing her fully to his gaze. There was nothing he couldn't see with her bent over the bike like that; her full buttocks still lightly marked from the spanking earlier, her red, swollen pussy glistening with her juices. He slid one finger along the inside of her slick thigh, then cupped her sex in his palm. She was ripe for him. His index finger found her swollen nub and flicked it; she moaned.

Frantically, he undid his own pants, freeing his cock, before landing another harsh slap to her ass. She mewled, lifting her hips slightly, offering herself to him. Damn, she was gorgeous.

Grabbing her hips, he slammed himself inside her, surging in to the hilt. She felt so good. Hot. Tight. Pulling out, he plunged back in again, taking her roughly, harshly. There was nothing gentle in his movements; it was aggression that drove him now. It was aggression that she needed; she pushed back against him, taking him in further, rocking in time with his movements.

A few more hard thrusts and he leaned back, his cock sitting just at her entrance, teasing her. He slapped her again, with his left hand this time, and watched in satisfaction as a dark pink handprint sprang up almost immediately. Marnie groaned beneath him, arching her back, silently pleading with him to fill her again.

"Do you want to come again, little girl?" he leaned down to growl in her ear.

"Yessir," she ground out between clenched teeth. "Please!"

Burying his cock deep inside her again, he grabbed a handful of her hair with his left hand, wrenching her head back, and slipped his right hand underneath her to touch her clit. She was trapped between his body and the bike, completely at his mercy. He liked it, he liked her helplessness. Her clit was pulsing; he rubbed it and she bucked beneath him.

"More."

Bringing his hand back, he tugged her hair sharply and landed another harsh slap to her rump. "You don't make the orders, little girl," he growled. "If you want to come, you stay there like that, bent over this bike, and wait for me to fuck you. On *my* terms."

"Yessir." Her reply was little more than a squeak this time; he could hear her submission. It nearly did him in.

This was so wrong. He shouldn't be doing this. He knew it. But at the same time, it felt so, so right.

• • • • • • •

Sam teased her mercilessly, filling her so completely then pulling out, leaving her empty and bereft. He kept his cock right there, at the entrance to her tight cunt, tormenting her, making her hot for him. Every fibre of her being wanted him. His huge palm whacked against her backside, stinging and burning, yet she wanted that, too. Right now, she was like putty in his hands.

She was dripping for him, she could feel it. His powerful body anchored her in place and drove his cock in deeper, driving her wild with desire. She was far from a virgin, but she'd never had sex like this before. It wasn't just the position that made it unique—bent over the back of a muddy farm bike—but it was the raw power emanating from the man behind her, the man fucking her senseless, claiming her body as his own, taking his pleasure.

His growly voice so close to her ear did wicked things to her. Heat surged to her core in response to his words, the stern tone twisting around inside her, and she offered her body to him in a wanton display of pure lust.

Their bodies moved in unison, a flawless dance, with each stinging slap of Sam's palm bringing her closer and closer to the edge. One more slap, one more thrust, and she'd tip over. His fingers moved against her clit again, touching her *right there*.

"Oh, my god. Sam!" She squealed his name as her body shuddered, overcome with racking spasms as the powerful orgasm ripped away any semblance of dignity she had left. The pleasure washed over her in waves, rocking through her body again and again, making her head spin and her insides explode. Sam was next to her, not touching her now, and she watched out of the corner of her eye as he spilled his hot seed on the ground.

Eventually, the waves of intense pleasure subsided and Marnie crashed back to reality. Beside her, Sam stood tucking his shirt into his pants, a sheepish grin on his face.

Fuck. What had she just done?

CHAPTER FOUR

So much for not screwing the crew. He'd only just managed to pull out in time. God. What if he'd managed to knock her up in hours of meeting her?

Marnie looked as shell-shocked as he felt. They'd both lost their heads, which was fine for her, a traumatized girl from a broken city, but what was his excuse?

She hadn't gotten up yet. Her legs were still wobbly. He could see the tremor in her thighs, and her pants were still down. He could see her well-fucked pussy, the wet folds of her sex. She'd felt incredible. Hot and tight, and so fucking wet. He felt his cock twitch again inside his jeans, but his head was clearer now. He knew what he wanted, and what he had to do.

She started to get up, but he reached out and pressed his hand down on the small of her back, keeping her in place.

"Stay."

She looked over her shoulder, and he saw confusion in her eyes. He had to make this right, make sure she knew he wasn't just pumping and dumping her.

"Let me up, Sam," she blushed.

"In a minute," he said, enjoying how cute she was with her face flushed from multiple orgasms, and the embarrassment of being out here in the open with her pussy on display. "I want to get a few things straight with you first, little girl."

She let out a little groan. "We just had sex, Sam, you can't call me that."

"Sure I can, they're two different things. You're a very attractive woman, Marnie, all grown up, no doubt about that." He slapped her ass lightly. "But I'm going to look after you too, and that means you're also my little girl. Get used to it."

"What? Like I don't have a choice?"

"After what we did? I don't think either of us have a choice, sweetheart. I don't know about you, but I don't usually fuck chicks I just met."

"I don't usually fuck chicks I just met either," she mumbled, squirming.

He snorted and smacked her ass again. "You know what I mean. We did what we did. It's going to happen again, so…"

"Is it?"

"You don't want to do that again?"

"I…" She trailed off, unable to finish her sentence.

She didn't want to admit it. He got that. Chicks were way harder on themselves when they had sex. Nobody was going to judge him for fucking her that quickly, but odds were she was already feeling guilty. She looked it. He wasn't going to let her slide into that state of mind.

"There's nothing wrong with what we just did," he said, his palm splayed across her ass, possessive. "We're both adults, we both wanted it."

• • • • • • •

Marnie's head was spinning. She couldn't believe what had just happened. She'd never had sex like that before. She'd never fucked a guy she hardly knew. She'd never been spanked to orgasm, and she had definitely never been held down afterward and given a talking to.

Her pussy was tender from the multiple orgasms, her butt was stinging from the spanking, and the way he was talking to her made her all quivery again. Sam liked to be in charge; that much was obvious. It had been apparent from the moment she met him, and it had come roaring out when he took her. She'd laid there and let him have her and called him sir and loved every second of it, and now he was telling her how it was going to be... her heart started to pound.

It wasn't that she wasn't safe with him. It was that she wasn't safe inside herself. What was happening? This wasn't her. She didn't jump guys she'd just met. She didn't fuck around. She didn't do this. She couldn't do this.

"Let me up, Sam. Now." This time there was a real strident borderline panic in her voice, and this time he listened.

He moved his hand and stood back.

"Don't freak out," he said in soothing tones. "It's okay."

"I'm not freaking out, I just want to get my pants on," she said, tugging them up so she could feel a little more equal, a little more in control of herself. Once she was covered, she ran a hand through her sex-tussled hair and addressed him directly to his chest.

"I'm not... I'm not a slut, Sam."

"I know you're not."

"No, you don't," she said. "Because I got off the bus and ended up on your dick." She turned around and looked away from him entirely. What the fuck was she doing? Who was she now? Is this what she did? Fuck.

Tears began to form in her eyes. She was so confused. She hadn't just fucked him. She'd... god. What was the word... she had *submitted* to him. She'd begged him to take her. She'd acted like she didn't have any morals or sense or anything. They hadn't even used a condom, and she hadn't cared about that either. His hot, bare cock had been thrusting inside her. He could have come inside her if he'd wanted. She wouldn't have stopped him. The thought made her tender pussy clench and her stomach do flips.

God! Get a grip! she lectured herself silently.

"You've been through a lot, Marnie," he said softly from behind her. "Maybe you just needed this. That's okay."

Earthquakes could be blamed for a lot of things, but she'd never heard of anyone turning into a total slut because of them.

Her shoulders shook as she started to cry from confusion and fear. Fear that she didn't know who she was and didn't know what she'd do next. Earthquakes had made the outside world unpredictable, and now she didn't even know herself.

Strong arms wrapped around her from behind, a large male chest against her back. He held her without speaking, seeming to know words would make it worse. She sniffled until the hot breeze took the tears away, until the calm of the countryside started to seep into her.

"Let me take care of you, Marnie," Sam murmured in her ear.

"I can't."

He turned her around gently and looked down at her with a quizzical expression. "What do you mean, you can't?"

"I mean…" She shook her head. "I just can't, Sam, I'm sorry."

"Okay," he nodded. "That's okay."

She'd disappointed him. She'd disappointed herself.

"Really," he said, taking her by the chin and looking down into her eyes. "It's okay, Marnie. I'm not going to force you to do anything you don't want to do."

Except he hadn't had to force her. She'd thrown herself at him. "Let's just leave it, okay?"

"Okay," he said, letting go of her.

Marnie missed his touch immediately, wanted to dive back into his arms. She was starting to figure out part of what attracted her to him so much. Sam was the first person she'd met in ages who wasn't carrying massive stress. He was relaxed, and even when he was growling, he was in control of his domain. Control. She needed that so badly. Right now everything was out of control, including herself.

"You're tired," he said. "We can do the farm tour another time. Right now, I think you could do with a nap. Let's go back to the house."

It wasn't really a suggestion. It was an order, one she didn't feel inclined to refuse. He got back on the bike he'd just ravaged her over and told her to get on. She didn't argue. The ride back was an embarrassing reminder of everything that had just happened. Her tender pussy rubbed against her wet jean shorts, more chafing than tantalizing and every bump and rumble reminded her of what a slut she'd just been. Even having her arms wrapped around his hard, lean waist was an exquisite torture.

When they got back, she dumped the helmet, kicked her boots off on the doorstep, and practically ran into the house, up to the room he'd shown her to. She didn't get into bed, she just wrapped the blanket around herself and over her head and squeezed her eyes shut. She wasn't going to be able to sleep, but maybe she could escape the total mess she'd made of her life by staying in the soft blanket.

• • • • • • •

Several hours later, she woke up. Hungry.

The growling in her stomach led her downstairs, and her nose took her to the kitchen, where she found Sam standing next to the stove, stirring a pot of something that smelled amazing.

"Hey there," he smiled as she came in. "Feel better?"

He'd showered. It was the first thing she noticed. And he'd shaved. The hard lines of his jaw were even clearer now, and the cable knit Merino sweater he was wearing brought out the colour of his eyes. God. He was fucking handsome. Now she felt like a mess compared to him, still in her dusty, sticky shorts.

"Uhmmm… I should get cleaned up," she said, not

answering his question.

"Sure, the door opposite your room leads to a bathroom," he said. "Sorry, I should have shown you there first. There's clean towels in there too."

She noticed that he wasn't calling her little girl anymore. For the first time since they met he wasn't growling because she'd just tramped dirt through the house, or threatening her with a spanking for something or other. He was being polite and respectful and, well, normal. It was just what she'd been asking for, and it was terrible.

"What are you cooking?" It seemed such a trivial question after what they'd shared together, but she didn't know what else to say. And she had to say something, or she was going to scream.

Despite feeling gross, she didn't really want a shower. She wanted Sam. She wanted him to bend her over the kitchen bench and ravish her again, just as he'd done over the bike. She wanted to hear the words *little girl* rumble off his lips as his huge hands grabbed her ass and pulled her closer to his hard body. She didn't want him to just stand there, all clean and respectable, cooking, while she felt so confused and uncomfortable and dirty.

"Rice pudding."

"For dinner?"

A slow smile spread across Sam's face as he took in her surprised expression. "Why not? Add canned peaches... the best food in the world!"

Sam definitely didn't seem like a rice pudding and peaches kind of man. He seemed like a 'throw the chops on the barbie' kind of man, with mashed spuds and peas. Or the kind of man who could devour a steak bigger than her hand with ease. Rice pudding didn't seem macho enough for him.

"Besides, it's all I know how to cook. Aunty Magda usually cooks, fortunately, but she's not here. So it's either this, which tastes bloody good, or baked beans on toast, which is pretty average."

"Okay. I like rice pudding." Her approval of Sam's choice of cuisine seemed to please him—his smile widened as he stirred the contents of the pot rather enthusiastically.

"Your bag is upstairs. Should be beside your bedroom door, I took it up for you earlier. Get yourself cleaned up and changed; food's ready when you are."

She frowned at his bossiness. He seemed to thrive on giving orders, and even though he said it all with a smile, he spoke like what he said wasn't up for negotiation. Like he just expected she would obey.

"And if I don't want to?"

Sam shrugged. "Then don't."

Marnie's heart sank. Shouldn't he at least be frowning and flexing his hands menacingly? Where had the stern disciplinarian gone? Where was the man who had turned her over his knee and spanked her? This man, the man who didn't seem to care what she did... she didn't like him very much at all.

Turning on her heel, Marnie stomped back up the stairs, looking for the bathroom. If Sam wasn't going to react the way she'd hoped he would, she may as well do something about the dirt coating her legs, the shorts sticking to her thighs, and the dust coating her top. Ugh. She'd never been this dirty in her life! She flicked at a patch of muck sticking to her forearm. How did people survive out here with all this filth?

The bathroom was easy to find. It was dead opposite her bedroom, just as Sam said it was, and the door was wide open. The small room clearly hadn't been updated, probably ever. Reaching inside, she pulled the cord of the old-fashioned light switch and blinked rapidly, letting her eyes adjust to the light, as the single bare bulb illuminated the room. There wasn't much space to move in there; small bathrooms must have been all the rage when this place had been built. A huge claw-foot tub with a blue shower curtain hanging from a rail above it took up most of the space and beside it, a small wooden vanity unit stood. The lino, although clean, was stained and splotched and almost worn through in places. Not exactly fancy. She moved further into the room. A frosted glass window was wedged permanently open, presumably to let out the steam. *And to let in the cold*, her inner mind snarked. Hadn't they heard of extraction fans out here? Was it really preferable to freeze rather than modernize?

Pushing the door shut with her shoulder, Marnie turned the key in the lock. Immediately, her breath hitched in her throat and her airways seemed to swell with panic. With the door shut, the tiny room was claustrophobic and she felt trapped. After the earthquakes, trapped was something she definitely did not want to be. Terror built up inside her.

"Just breathe," she whispered. "You'll be okay. You'll be okay. You'll be okay." Maybe if she repeated the mantra often enough she'd start to believe it. Closing her eyes tight against the sensations pushing against her, she repeated it again. Several deep breaths later, her racing heart started to slow. She opened her eyes.

How the hell was she going to do this? How was she going to survive out here? She hated the dust, wasn't too excited about the job she didn't even know she had, and she was terrified of the bathroom.

But the boss is pretty cute, she reminded herself. *And the ground stays still out here. That's a definite bonus.*

Standing next to it, the bath was even bigger than she'd first thought: the top of it came up to her mid-thigh and it was much longer than she was tall. Sam would probably be able to stretch right out inside it. *Don't think about Sam*, she chided herself. *He fucked you and discarded you. He's gone all polite on you—won't even threaten you with a spanking. Don't even go there.*

A blue rubber mat with sucky feet sat in the base of the bath directly under the showerhead, just in front of the plug. Rust circled the drain but the tub itself was clean, even free from the infernal dust that seemed to coat everything out here. Inside the vanity unit, behind the cupboard door that didn't quite shut, were clean towels, rolled up, sitting in neat rows. The bright, organized towels looked as out of place in the dingy room as she felt. Pulling the top one from the pile, she clutched it to her chest, finding comfort in the familiar smell of Persil that still lingered in the fluffy threads. Had Sam used this towel before? It was big; she could imagine him wrapping it around his body, soaking up the water droplets that clung to his muscular chest. She'd felt enough of his body while on the bike to know that he was ripped, she didn't need to actually see him shirtless to picture what he would look like wearing nothing but this towel... her pussy tightened at the image and her clit throbbed. Discarding the towel, she tore off her clothes.

Marnie felt herself relaxing under the fine mist of the warm shower. The tension slowly left her body as she turned her back into the spray, letting the warm water trickle over her shoulders and down her back. She wished it was Sam's fingers gently massaging away her stress.

It felt good to get clean again. She dragged the soap over her thighs, between her legs, washing away the final remnants of Sam. Sparks shot through her as she remembered the way Sam's cock had felt buried inside her, the way he'd filled her so completely and fucked her so hard, but it wasn't enough. She wanted more; a primal, carnal need welled up within her, making her feel like a wanton little hussy. Short, quick breaths signalled her arousal at the memory.

Her own fingers brushed over taut nipples. Had Sam touched there, too? She couldn't remember; sparks had been everywhere. If he hadn't, she wanted him to.

She trailed the soap down her torso, wishing it was Sam's fingers, not the soap, washing her body.

By her calculations, the kitchen was directly below her. Sam was directly below her. If he could look up from the pot he was stirring, through the floorboards, and see what she was doing, see how horny the memories of his ministrations were making her, what would he think?

With great effort, she dragged her mind away from Sam.

She was being ridiculous. He was just a man. A very sexy, very bossy, very much man, but just a man. *Just a man who presses all the right buttons, you mean*, her inner voice tormented her. *And when have you ever had a man like Sam?*

The light went out.

Marnie's terrified scream echoed around the small room, bouncing off the walls and adding to her confusion. It took her a couple of seconds to realize what the noise was. She shut her mouth. She'd heard enough screams lately to last her for a lifetime. But although she was silent, her heart pounded, her hands were clenched into tight fists of fear, and every muscle in her body was taut, ready to run.

It wasn't dark; enough light from the twilight outside came in the window that she could see, but the sudden outage of the light compounded with the claustrophobia of the tiny room. She could barely breathe.

Heavy, rushing footsteps sounded on the stairs outside. *Sam.* Had she screamed that loud? Shame flooded her as she realized that indeed, she had. What would he think of her now? She didn't even have to try very hard to imagine the derision she knew would be written all over his face. And she was naked, so that already put her at a disadvantage. Huddling pathetically under the warm water, she wished the drain was big enough to swallow her down, make her disappear.

"Marnie?" Sam pounded on the door.

Thank god she'd locked it. The last thing she needed was for Sam to come barging in.

At that moment, as suddenly as it had gone off, the bulb flicked back on, flooding the room with light once again. Marnie breathed a sigh of relief.

"Are you okay?" Sam called.

She took a breath, willing her racing heart to slow and her rapid breathing to steady enough for her to speak. She was panicked, her body in flight mode.

"I'm okay," she ground out through clenched teeth.

"Open the door."

"No, I'm fine!"

"You were screaming. Open it. Now." She could hear the tension in his voice. He wasn't asking, he was demanding.

"I'll be out in a bit!"

"Now, little girl."

She couldn't help the grin that spread over her face as she heard him say that, even just as a gruff disembodied voice through the door. She still hadn't moved though. The shower was running, water dribbling over her back and shoulders.

"Do I have to get a screwdriver and open this?" Sam's voice came again.

"Hold on! I'm coming!"

She turned the water off, rubbed the towel over her hair and then wrapped it around her body before going to the door and opening it. She found herself looking up into his worried face.

"The light went out," she explained before he had a chance to ask. "I got a fright."

He looked at her sceptically. "You screamed like you were dying."

"Yeah, well, turns out I wasn't," she said, giving him a sarcastic thumbs-up.

Sam looked at her in a way she didn't like, as if he didn't quite believe her.

"The light went out. I got a fright. I made a little bit of a noise," she said. "I'm fine."

• • • • • • •

Marnie had just gotten out of the shower, so she was pink around the ears and nose, but she still looked pale to Sam. And that scream, it hadn't been one of shock. It had been one of pure fear. He'd felt it bolting down his spine, ringing in his ears even all the way downstairs.

She said she had been frightened by the light going off.

He believed that. It could be a bit dodgy at times, but most people didn't scream their lungs out over it. Was she that afraid of the dark?

He wanted to push it further, but she'd been clear back in the paddock. She wanted her space, and he was going to give it to her. He was a lot of things, but he didn't force himself on women who didn't want what he had to offer.

"Alright," he said. "Well, dinner's ready when you are."

He turned around and heard her huff.

"Drag me out of the shower just for that," she complained.

He glanced over his shoulder. "Hmm?"

"I mean, come on, Sam. Do you come running every time you hear a little squeak? You force me out of the shower just to answer to you? I told you I was fine."

What was she doing? Was she baiting him? His palms were tingling with desire to yank that towel right off her and spank her bare bottom, but he was still respecting her earlier request for him to leave her be and not try to take care of her.

He walked toward the stairs, knowing full well there wasn't an answer she wanted to hear.

"Dick."

The word was uttered behind him in rebellious tones.

"Okay, that's enough." He turned around and faced her as she stood pouting in the towel. "I was worried about you. I came up to check. No need to be rude."

"Fine. Check. But I told you I was okay through the door."

They were glowering at each other now. She was mad, and he didn't think it was because he'd asked her to open the door. This was obviously about the sex. That had been a really big mistake. Not that he regretted it, but it seemed like she did.

"What do you want, Marnie? Do you want me to spank you? Is that it?"

"No," she said hoarsely, her fingers twisting in the towel.

The longer she was out of the shower, the paler she looked. He noticed that she was breathing faster than she really should have been, and there was a tremor in her hands as she adjusted the towel. Her pupils were dilated too, her nostrils flaring. If she were a horse, she'd be about to bolt.

"Marnie," he said, softening his tone. "What's wrong?"

"Nothing," she insisted.

"Don't lie to me, little girl."

• • • • • • •

"God! Just leave me alone, Sam!"

Marnie was asking for the one thing she really didn't want at all. Actually, she didn't ask for it. She shouted it. At full volume.

She didn't want him to leave her alone, but she didn't want to admit what was going on either. She was melting down, that's what was happening. She was freaking the fuck out, for no reason other than the bathroom was too small and the light had gone out and now she really, really needed someone to hold her.

"That's it," he growled, advancing on her.

She expected him to grab her and smack her. What she didn't expect was to be picked up over his shoulder in one swooping motion and be carried into her bedroom, the towel that had somewhat protected her modesty left behind on the bathroom floor.

"Sam! No!"

He sat down on the bed, slid her naked body down from his shoulder, and pulled her into his lap. Not over it, thank god. His big arms wrapped around her, and his fingers found her chin, forcing her to look into his steel blue eyes.

"That is not the way to get me to leave you alone, little girl," he growled.

She felt her breath catching in her throat as she looked at him. She was naked! He didn't seem to care about that though. He had lecturing to do, and he was obviously going to do it.

"Is that really what you want? Because right now you're doing everything to make me whip your ass as long and as hard as I can."

Marnie shrank down in his arms. She had a sense of his strength, and knew he was capable of carrying out the threat. She might be in real trouble now.

"No," she whispered.

"Then tell me what's going on."

"I got scared," she mumbled.

"Because the light went out?" His voice was softer now, more encouraging. There was none of the judgment and disdain she'd feared.

"Because I freak out sometimes," she mumbled, tears coming into her eyes as she told him the last thing she wanted to admit. "I just... get scared for no reason. Ever since the quake. It's so stupid. I hate it."

His arms tightened around her, snuggling her close against his powerful male body. She felt the soft knit of his sweater against her naked curves, his pants a little rough against her bare bottom.

"The quakes must have been really scary," he said, speaking softly, his deep voice soothing her. "Sometimes, when something really scary happens, your body remembers it for a long time afterward. It's not stupid."

"Yes, it is," she said, trying her best not to cry. "Because I came here, and I was so stupid I didn't even know what I was supposed to be doing and then you yelled at me because I don't know about horses, and I slept with you and... I'm so dumb!"

"You are not dumb," he rumbled as she started to cry. "You're stressed and you're tired and I've given you a harder time than I should have. I'm sorry. And I'm sorry about what happened over the bike..."

Marnie started to cry even harder. He wished he hadn't slept with her. She didn't blame him. "It's my fault, I know I'm gross. You must think I'm such a stupid slut."

"Don't you dare talk about yourself that way!" Sam's censure snapped her out of her self-pity. "I don't mean I'm sorry about what we did. I'm sorry that we did it so quickly, before you even had a chance to settle or get to know me. I should have waited. It would have been better for you, but I wanted you, so I took you."

His words made her quiver low in her belly. Yes. He had taken her. He had taken her and she had forgotten about everything except him. For the first time in weeks and weeks, she'd actually been free of the stress of the earthquakes and everything she'd lost. Her tears dried as she remembered how he'd held her down, fucked her thoroughly and then kept her in place, displaying her pussy to the world. She wished she hadn't told him to let her up. She wished they could do it again. Now. Her nakedness, which had been so shameful at first, was starting to become an advantage. There was nothing to stop him from pulling his cock out and pushing it inside her again, fucking her until she forgot about the very concept of fear.

"Sam..." she said his name huskily. "I wanted you too."

"I know," he said, shifting her a little on his lap, moving her just the barest fraction away from his crotch. "But I want to take my time with you, Marnie. You deserve that. You need time to adjust to things here. And there's a lot of adjusting to do. I'm not an easy man to work for, let alone to be with..."

"Yeah," she said with a little giggling snort. "I reckon!"

"Right, so, let's get you dressed," he said, sliding her onto the bed.

She sat there, pouting as he retrieved her suitcase and slid it up onto a small chest of drawers, sliding the zippers open. She thought about complaining about her privacy, but as he reached into the suitcase and pulled out a pair of panties with pink hearts on them and turned to her with a smile, she didn't think she cared very much about her privacy anymore.

"Legs out," he said, crouching in front of her.

"You're not going to dress me, Sam." She blushed incredulously down at the handsome man with the brilliant blue eyes who was handling her underwear.

"Oh, yes, I am, little girl," he rumbled, sliding one leg of the panties over her raised foot as she offered it in spite of her objections. "And then we're going to go and eat some tea."

Marnie held his gaze as Sam slid the underwear up her legs, his fingers brushing the inside of her thighs as he raised them higher. She wiggled her hips, trying to brush her pussy accidentally-on-purpose across his fingers. It didn't work. Instead, Sam frowned as he pulled her to her feet and gently put the underwear in place, snugging the elastic firm around her hips.

"Right. Pyjamas."

"I don't want to wear pyjamas," she protested. "It's not night-time yet!"

"Pyjamas are just what you need, little girl," Sam insisted in a gravelly voice. "We're not going back outside today; we're going to have dinner, sign your employment contract, then go to bed. We have an early start in the morning, remember."

Marnie groaned. She hadn't forgotten, but she was hoping he had. Or that he was at least going to ease her into it gently. Getting up at half past five in the morning would be akin to torture.

While he was turned around fishing in her suitcase for more clothing, Marnie glared at his back. She remembered how nice it had been pressed up against that same broad back on the bike, how strong it had felt. She felt herself blush even more as she remembered what had happened on that bike and what had come straight afterward. She wanted to do it again. She *really* wanted to do it again.

Smiling mischievously, she pouted her lips just slightly, in the way that she knew made her look sexy, then folded her arms across her ribcage, just under her breasts, the pressure of her arms thrusting her breasts up and out, making her bosom look far more impressive than it actually was.

"These ones?" Sam held up a pair of pink flannel pyjamas with black cats on them and turned to her. His eyes widened as he automatically glanced at her chest, holding the pyjamas out in front of him, sort of like a shield. Like he was protecting himself from something... from her. Quickly, he looked away, perhaps trying to pretend that her pose, the one she was putting on especially for him, didn't affect him at all. But it did; she'd seen his reaction, the way his eyes had burned with lust, the rather large bulge tenting the front of his jeans. She smiled smugly. He wanted her; good.

"Those ones," she confirmed.

It was a bit embarrassing, having a man handling her sleepwear. Especially when the only sleepwear she'd thought to pack was so childish, in stark contrast to the skimpy clothes she'd been wearing all day. If she'd known someone as sexy as Sam would be seeing her night attire she would have found a sexy sheer lace nightie to wear or something, not the comfy, worn PJs she'd had for years—a birthday present from Grandma. Although, if she were honest, she hadn't actually been thinking too much at all when she'd stuffed the only clothes she could find into the suitcase. She hadn't really considered what she might need, and most of her stuff had been destroyed by the liquefaction anyway. Her favourite pyjamas were probably lucky to escape the oozing muddy liquid that covered nearly everything else.

Sam was so close she could hear him breathing, the raspy inhalations coming in a quick, shallow rhythm. He was so close she could stretch out her hand just the tiniest bit and run her fingers up the front of his thigh. Sparks zinged between his jeans and her fingertips, her skin on fire as she worked her way slowly up his leg, angling inward, toward his crotch. The hard muscles of his thigh rippled beneath her touch. He sucked in a breath. He felt so good beneath her hand. It felt so right to touch him on her terms, rather than the other way round. It occurred to her then that this was the first time she had touched him voluntarily. She'd been in his arms, she'd hung on around his waist on the back of the motorbike, and she'd been across his knee getting her butt smacked, but touching him now, feeling his body beneath her hand, in control, was entirely different. Electricity bolted through her, tingling her spine, setting her nerve endings on fire.

Her fingers rested at the base of his fly, just briefly, then she spread out her hand, cupping his balls in her palm, feeling the weight of them even through his jeans. She squeezed lightly. He froze.

"No." Sam's voice was hoarse as he grabbed her wrist and held it away from him, his palm clammy, his fingers far too tight around her. He swallowed, his Adam's apple bobbing. "No. Get dressed."

Tears of rejection pricked behind her eyes and she felt her face flame. "You don't want me," she whispered, barely able to hold herself together. But she would not cry. Not now. Not because of him.

"Oh, I definitely want you, little girl," Sam growled. "But I need to do what's best for you."

"You don't know what's best for me."

• • • • • • •

What the hell was he doing? He shouldn't be here, he shouldn't be doing this. He shouldn't be in her room with her, especially not when she was mostly naked, her forearm hoisting up her beautiful breasts, making them look even more voluptuous and tempting.

She was right: he didn't know what was best for her. If he did, they wouldn't be in this situation right now. She wouldn't be sitting mostly naked on the bed and he wouldn't be holding her pyjamas, having just slid her knickers up her thighs and over her hips, hiding her most intimate places from his view. He could still see her in his memory though, the glistening folds of her pussy, wet for him, pink and swollen with arousal.

The gentle slide of his fingers up his leg nearly did him in. He knew what she was doing, the little brat—her intention was written plainly all over her face. She was trying to seduce him, and a damn fine job she was doing of it, too! But he couldn't let her. Not after what he'd done to her on the bike. He still wanted to kick himself for taking advantage of her like that. Not that he regretted their fucking, but he should have known better. He *did* know better. Aunty Magda would have his guts for garters if she knew he was treating the new hand in that way. And judging by the utterly devastated look on Marnie's face right now, he'd not only ripped her heart out when he'd pulled her hand away from him, but he'd trampled on it, too. Knowing how much he'd hurt her made him feel worse.

He needed a cold shower. He needed to do something, *anything*, to get the thoughts of the beautiful blonde sitting on the bed in front of him out of his head. She wasn't his plaything, she wasn't his girlfriend. She was his new employee. What kind of asshole was he, giving into temptation so quickly?

"I'm sorry, Marnie, I really am."

"Fuck off." It was a snarl, but filled with pain.

"You wanted me to leave you alone," he reminded her gently.

"Maybe I've changed my mind?" she yelled at him, tears streaming down her face now, but her voice strong. "You can't really be that much of an idiot, can you? I've changed my mind!"

As close as she'd been to making him lose control with her seduction, the sudden petulance was not a turn-on. At all. He didn't sleep with women because they cried and demanded it. Marnie was tired and stressed, but there was no excuse for this behaviour whatsoever. She'd been disrespectful from the beginning, and he was about done with it.

"Don't speak to me like that, Marnie."

"Like what? Calling you an idiot? That's what you are. An idiot! A stupid damn dumbass!"

"Get dressed," he said, his tone clipped. "Now."

"No!"

She didn't pick up on his change of tone, or if she did, she didn't sense the warning. Either way, Sam was done arguing with this bratty little girl.

He grabbed Marnie and proceeded to physically wrestle her into her pyjamas. She cursed and swore and squirmed as he pulled the top over her head, resisting him while he did his best to push her arms into the sleeves. She was acting like the little girl he described her as being, and not in any kind of charming or sweet way. She was a little hellion in dire need of proper discipline. His palm caught her deserving bottom several times, painting the soft flesh outside her panties with bright red fingerprints. When her top was on, he pinned her on her back on the bed using his body weight, pulled the pyjama pants up and over her feet and legs, and yanked them firmly into place.

Marnie yelled blue murder throughout the whole proceedings. Anyone would have thought she was being tortured. Never in his life had Sam seen anyone fuss this much over putting their clothes on. If she put half the energy she put into resisting him into paying attention and learning her new job, she'd pick it up in no time.

She was finally dressed, but he wasn't done with her. Not by a long way. Now he could turn her over his knee and give her what she really needed, and that's exactly what he did. Before she could mouth off yet again, he yanked her up from the bed and pulled her over his thigh, locking her legs between his legs by closing the other one. This wasn't going to be any warning ass warming. This was going to be the real thing.

"You want to sleep with me, Marnie?" he lectured, his palm meeting her ass firmly. "You behave yourself. You do as you're told. You don't swear and scream and yell at me like a spoiled little girl."

"Why not! You keep calling me that!"

He laid into her then, his palm meeting her butt a good dozen times. He'd tried to ease her into this gently, but Marnie just kept pushing. No matter what he did, she acted out. She'd probably hate him for this too, but he'd rather she hated him for this than let her carry on thinking that shit was going to fly.

The sound of his hand meeting her ass was like gunshots echoing around the room, followed by the higher pitched plaintive cries that escaped her with every swat. She was still noisy, but at least she wasn't swearing and yelling at him anymore. She was too busy getting thoroughly spanked. Her gasps and yelps sounded perfect to his ears, just the right blend of shocked and plaintive.

Hopefully she was learning her lesson and he wouldn't have to hear her call him a dick again. And what else had she called him? Idiot. That's right. Letting out a little growl, he hooked his hand in the back of her pyjamas and panties, pulling them down just below her ass. Her cheeks were an even pink colour. Good start, but not nearly enough. He set about making it a proper red, whipping his palm against her cheeks over and over until her toes drummed against the floor.

Marnie wasn't going to curse at him again. She wasn't going to call him disrespectful names. She wasn't going to just demand sex as if he were her personal fuck toy. This little girl had a lot to learn about a lot of things, especially about him.

"When I tell you to do something, you do it," he lectured as she writhed over his lap. "You don't answer back. You don't call me a dick. You sure as hell don't refuse to put your clothes on. As for the rest—I'll let you know when I'm ready to fuck you again, Marnie. Understand?"

She didn't answer. She was too busy snivelling.

He smacked her bare ass hard. "I said, understand?"

"Yes!" She squealed the word.

"Good."

He held her in place, one hand fisted in the back of her pyjamas, the other resting on her hot ass. It looked perfect like this, two squirming red rounds and the little cleft between them where he knew she would be hot and wet. His lust rose, but he pushed it back down. Now wasn't the time.

"Get up," he said, pulling her to her feet. There were tears running down her pretty face. She looked at him with a wounded, doe-like expression. That didn't please him either. There was no need for her to be feeling sorry for herself. She hadn't been hard done by. This was what brats got. As far as he was concerned, she was damn lucky he hadn't taken his belt off for her.

"Go stand in the corner."

"What?"

He got up, grabbed her by the back of the collar, and marched her into the corner of the room. He pushed her firmly into it so her nose was pressed against the very apex, then took her hands and put them on top of her head.

"They stay there, and your butt stays bare until I say so," he told her. "Move a centimetre and we'll start all over again."

She didn't move. She stood there sniffling to herself as he took a step back, folding his arms over his chest. He had a good mind to send her to bed without tea, but she needed to eat, and doing so on a sore bottom might be a decent reminder of how to speak to him.

Not yet though. For now she was going to stand there like the brat she was, her bright red ass on satisfying display. Sam rubbed his hands together, easing some of the sting out of them. His palm probably ached about as much as her little butt did.

He checked his watch. Fifteen minutes should do it. Then he'd see if she'd learned a damn thing. He sat back down on the bed, took a load off his feet, keeping an eye on her.

"Don't," he said sharply as she adjusted her hand, looking like she might be about to move.

As silence settled over the room for the first time in quite a few minutes, Sam got to enjoy the sight of Marnie's shapely rear on display. She was a pretty girl. Very pretty, actually. Weren't many girls like her out here in the country. Weren't many girls, full stop. Might not be for long either. He wouldn't be surprised if she packed her bags and left after this. That would be her choice, but he couldn't have an undisciplined brat around the place. Horse trekking could be dangerous work, and someone who lost their temper and started screaming when they didn't get their way had no place in it.

• • • • • • •

Marnie stayed very, very still.

Her ass was burning. She could feel her cheeks twitching periodically, little spasms of the muscle beneath her spanked skin as it reacted to the thrashing he'd just given her.

Emotionally, shock didn't begin to cover the way she felt. She still couldn't believe it. One minute she had been arguing with him, the next he was whipping her ass. Maybe she shouldn't be shocked. He had threatened to do that, and it had been just like he promised it would be. It had been hard. And it had hurt.

She hated him. The way he'd manhandled her into her pyjamas then flipped her over so effortlessly and branded her with searing, scorching smacks that seemed to go on forever... she was stunned. What else would he do to hurt her? If she was honest with herself, she was scared of him, too. More than just a little bit scared. She'd never been scared of a person before. Situations, yes. Spiders, yes. But people? No, people had never scared her. No man had ever enforced his will on her before, no man had ever taken her across his knee and spanked her soundly. And no one had ever punished her before for being upset, feeling hurt and rejected. But Sam had.

His harsh "don't!" when she'd tried to scratch the itch on the back of her head had made her tremble with fear and reinforced what a brute he was. If she had anywhere else to go, she would leave here, and go there. Aunt Elsie, her last surviving family member, had gone on a Caribbean cruise instead of hanging around Christchurch and fighting with the insurance company over her decimated house. She'd be gone for months. Marnie was all alone in the world. And to make matters worse, her bottom hurt.

She sniffed loudly. This wasn't fair! The earthquake had turned her entire life on its head, and she didn't like it one little bit.

Her legs were beginning to cramp and her arms were starting to ache from being held up in the air for so long. It felt like she'd been standing there forever. It was humiliating, being there like that, her bare ass on display to him. The stinging in her bottom hadn't abated any, but after so many minutes of having a burning butt, she was getting used to that. It was the standing still in the corner that she was struggling with the most. But she was too scared to move. She couldn't handle another spanking. Not after the way Sam had just laid into her, using what she was sure was close to his full strength to smack her bare, vulnerable ass. Did he like her like this? Sore and small?

"You can come out."

She flinched at his words, emerging unexpectedly from the silence. She didn't want to come out. She was safe where she was. He wasn't in the corner. She didn't have to look at him and see him looking at her.

Marnie felt his hands on her shoulders and stiffened as he turned her around gently. She looked studiously at the floor, and when he put his fingers beneath her chin, she resisted lifting her head.

"Marnie."

She bit her lower lip. She was not going to cry. She was

not going to look at him. She was just... not.

"Marnie." He said her name more firmly. Her shoulders hunched as she pulled her arms from her head and crossed them over her chest, protecting herself.

"Look at me."

She shook her head and kept her eyes on her toes.

She didn't want to look at him. She didn't want to talk to him. What was there to say? Besides, if she opened her mouth now, for all she knew he'd start whacking her again. Or maybe he'd start smacking her because she wouldn't look at him. She didn't know.

"Pull your pants up."

That was one order she was happy to follow. She dipped down and yanked her pants up, letting out an involuntary squeak as the fabric met her sore ass.

"Come on," he said. "You need to eat."

She wasn't hungry, but she followed him down the stairs, still refusing to make eye contact with him. Fortunately his back was to her until they got to the kitchen, though she didn't like looking at that either. Just reminded her how much more powerful than her he was.

Sam grabbed a cushion from the couch in the nearby lounge and put it down on one of the kitchen chairs. "Sit."

Marnie lowered herself gingerly into the chair. Sitting was not comfortable. Her ass throbbed with her weight on it, but the cushion made it a little easier. She sat there silently, looking at the table until Sam put a bowl of rice pudding and warm peaches in front of her. She didn't feel hungry.

"Eat."

She didn't want to make him angry, so she took a spoonful. It tasted pretty good, but she wasn't in the mood to appreciate cooking, good or otherwise. She chewed slowly, keeping her eyes on the bowl of food. Every swallow was a dry gulp. She would have liked some water, but she wasn't going to ask him for it.

Sam took a seat next to her, and for the next few minutes

the only sounds in the room were the clink of spoons in old ceramic bowls. Marnie sat there on her spanked bottom and tried to pretend that everything was normal. But it wasn't. It wasn't normal now, and it wouldn't ever be again. Eventually, she just couldn't pretend anymore. She let the spoon drop into the bowl as her tears threatened to fall.

"How could you do that to me?" Her lower lip trembled as she asked the question.

Sam reached over, his large hand covering hers as she stared at a half-eaten peach. The touch of his callused skin was more comforting than it should have been.

"You were screaming at me, Marnie. You were melting down. Calling me names. Did you expect to get away with that?"

"I don't know."

"You do know," he replied. "So tell me. Did you expect that to slide?"

"Yes," she admitted. "I did. I expected you to yell back at me, or call me an idiot too or something… but what you did was so much worse!"

"Was it? You'd rather I called you names than corrected your behaviour? You'd rather I lost my temper and yelled at you?"

"No," she mumbled as she pulled her hand away. "I guess not."

He sat back in his chair, spreading his legs and lacing his fingers together between his long thighs. He was so sure of himself. That was the strangest thing of all about this. He didn't seem guilty or sorry or anything.

"It's alright if you hate me," he said calmly.

"Well, thanks, Mr. Feelings Police."

She felt the sharp look he shot her without having to see it. It made her tingle all the way down to her toes. "Go on up to bed," he said. "Before you get yourself into more trouble."

She stood up and prepared to flee the kitchen.

"Marnie… one thing…"

She turned, wondering what he wanted. His arms extended around her and he drew her into a tight hug. She was pulled against the hard lines of his strong body, his long arms wrapped around her smaller frame as he rubbed her back with slow, calming circles she told herself she definitely didn't like, even as the tension began to drain from her shoulders and spine.

"I did that for your own good," he murmured into her hair. "But I didn't like upsetting you or hurting you that way. Get some sleep. I'll see you in the morning."

He released her and she turned and made for the stairs, still sulky, but feeling a little lighter.

For once, Marnie did exactly as she was told. She climbed up to the bedroom and crawled into bed. She hoped she could sleep with a sore ass. Sometimes she had trouble sleeping, sometimes…

The moment her head hit the pillow, she was out like a light.

CHAPTER FIVE

Sharp rapping on the door woke Marnie up. She groaned, blinking quickly trying to see in the dim light of the early morning but didn't move. Dawn had just broken, but to her it was still night-time.

"Marnie! Time to get up!" Sam's voice was muffled through the door, but he sounded firm. And after what he'd done to her last night, she wasn't inclined to disobey him quite so soon. Tomorrow, maybe, if her ass had recovered, but not just yet.

"Yeah, yeah, I'm coming," she mumbled.

Slowly, the door slid open and Sam strolled in, fully clothed, looking as chirpy as ever. She hated people like that; people who looked happy and alive first thing in the morning. People like that made her feel useless and lazy when she wasn't, not really. She just didn't like mornings. And in her experience, mornings didn't like her, either.

The bed dipped as Sam sat down on the edge of it. Marnie froze. Her stomach clenched as she remembered what had happened the last time Sam had sat in that very spot. It hadn't been pleasant in the least. She groaned again. "What time is it?"

"Five-thirty," Sam responded cheerily.

Marnie didn't move. Instead, she clutched the sheets tighter to her chest, a protective measure in case Sam decided to flip her over and smack her bottom again, just as he'd done last night. What had he told her yesterday, at the barn? Something about dragging her out of bed and slapping her ass before sending her down to breakfast? She sat up.

"Are you going to thrash me again?"

Sam's brow lowered just a fraction as he frowned at her. "Have you been naughty already? The day has barely begun!"

"No! I just mean…"

Marnie bounced in the bed as Sam stood up abruptly. "Five minutes, Marnie, don't be late."

She poked her tongue out at his retreating back, but slowly slid back the covers and got out of bed. Her ass was still sore and the skin felt tight. No way could she handle another spanking. She would be a good girl, for today at least.

• • • • • • •

He heard the floor creak in her bedroom as he sauntered back down the narrow stairs. Marnie was obviously getting out of bed. That was good. He smiled. She was so cute still half-asleep, the way she'd looked up at him with sleepy eyes, pink marks along her cheek from the creases in the sheet, her hair all tousled. She looked sweet and innocent and harmless, just like a kitten. And then she'd opened her mouth. She was going to be a handful.

The pipes under the sink clunked in protest when he turned the tap on to fill up the kettle. It really was time something was done about the plumbing in the house. It was far too temperamental for Sam's liking. Clicking the full kettle into the electric base, Sam flicked the switch to turn it on. No doubt Marnie would want coffee, and he could do with a cup himself. He didn't always start his mornings off with coffee, but with Marnie tagging alongside him all day today, he figured he would need all the help he could get.

He wanted to work with the young horses today, and it would be good for Marnie to watch. Maybe he could set her up in the yard with Taxi and the grooming bucket, get her used to horses slowly. She'd be safe with Taxi, nothing bothered him, and she'd be close enough to Sam for him to keep a bit of an eye on. He felt a bit guilty, throwing her into the deep end so quickly, but he had to get these young ones up to speed before the season kicked in fully. There were a few treks booked in this weekend, but it wouldn't get really busy until December. He needed Marnie, and the young horses, confident and capable by then.

Sam looked at his watch. She was cutting it a bit fine— forty-five seconds to go. He didn't exactly want to start the day off with a spanking, particularly not after being so hard on her last night, but he would if he had to. Marnie had to learn that he wasn't mucking around; when he said something, he expected to be obeyed. When the season got busy, he wouldn't have the time to be hovering over her, enforcing his orders. He had to be able to trust her.

With just five seconds remaining on the five-minute deadline, Marnie came clomping down the stairs. She'd tied her hair back; that was a good start. Long, loose hair had the potential to be dangerous around horses—if it got caught in a piece of tack and the horse took off, it could be very painful indeed. But that was about the only thing she'd done right. She was wearing the same short shorts again, and another tank top. Did she have no idea how strong the sun was out here? She'd be burned to a crisp if she didn't cover up a bit better than that. He was about to open his mouth to chide her choice of clothing, when he clamped it closed. He'd promised her just yesterday that he wouldn't do that. He'd also promised to take her to Farmlands, get her sorted clothes-wise. Dammit, he'd just have to tie Taxi up in the shade.

• • • • • • •

Marnie trailed the brush she was holding down the shoulder of the big brown gelding, Taxi, that Sam had tied to the railing. She'd been terrified, at first, standing next to a horse that was taller than her, but Taxi hadn't moved at all, he just stood there contentedly nibbling on his hay net. Slowly, she'd relaxed, and rummaged through the tack bucket Sam had left for her. He'd pointed out the dirt crusted to Taxi's coat that needed to come off, quickly showed her what to do, and then left her to it. Apparently, he had young horses to work. And from where she was standing, mostly hidden behind the gentle giant of a horse, she had the perfect vantage point.

She'd been out of bed for about an hour now, and she was still surprised by how well she was coping. The early morning air seemed so much fresher than normal and the grass was still damp with dew. And, most surprising of all, she wasn't even tired. It was somehow nice, being outside before there was too much heat in the sun, breathing in the scent of horseflesh. And that surprised her, too. Yesterday, the dirt and dust had horrified her. The stench of horses had disgusted her, and the thought of being so up close and personal to one of the big beasts had terrified her. But she was quickly learning that Taxi wasn't terrifying at all. He just stood there, totally ignoring her, while she half-heartedly swiped the brush at the dirt embedded in his shiny brown coat.

If she stepped sideways just a bit, she could see Sam working with one of the young horses. She had no idea what he was doing, but there was a lot of rope swinging going on, a fair bit of moving on the horse's part, and Sam's rumbly voice sounded pleased as he talked quietly to the horse. Her insides somersaulted; he'd used that same tone with her, once. And when he did, she'd been like putty in his hands. It had washed over her, infiltrating her, flowing through her pores, making her feel like the most important person in the world. It had turned her inside out and upside down, making her want to do scandalous things to him, and have him do scandalous things to her in return. *Like what he did on the bike…*

"How's it going?" Sam's deep voice interrupted her daydream and she jumped, startled. Beside her, Taxi didn't bat an eyelid.

"Um, yeah, okay I guess," she mumbled, refusing to meet his eyes. Did he know what she'd been thinking about? His timing was too perfect. She felt her face flush with heat. She had to stop thinking about that! Sam had made it clear that there would be no more sexual activity between them, and the way he'd rebuffed her advances last night still stung.

Sam took the brush from her hand and stroked it vigorously along Taxi's body, down his neck, across his ribcage, sending dust flying. "You have to put a bit of effort into it if you want to get the dirt out," he told her. "Like this. See?" A flick of his wrist sent a clump of horse hair and dried-on mud flying in Marnie's direction.

"Bleurgh!" Marnie coughed and fanned a hand in front of her face. He'd done that on purpose.

"Sorry." Sam chuckled. He didn't look sorry, though; far from it. If anything, he looked amused, seeing her choke on dust. "Here." He thrust the brush back at her. "I want to work with Trixie now. You just stay here with Taxi, get yourself acquainted with him, be confident around him. Brush his other side, too. We want both sides clean, not just one."

"Dick," she mumbled, half under her breath, as Sam walked away. "He's so arrogant!" she muttered to Taxi. "And so condescending!" The horse ignored her. "And bossy!" At that, Taxi snorted into his hay net, sending more dust, along with bits of hay, flying at her.

Marnie glared at the horse. "Great. Just great. You, too?"

If she hadn't turned right at that moment, she would have missed it, and Sam taking his shirt off, the fabric riding up his torso exposing the best six-pack she'd ever seen, was a not-to-be-missed sight. He was spectacular. His bare abs were well-defined, enhanced by the line of dark hair that trailed from his navel, down the centre of his body, and disappeared inside the waistband of his jeans. Her mouth watered. At that moment he turned to her and caught her ogling, then he threw the shirt at the fence, pulled his singlet down to cover his stomach and winked rakishly. Her heart skipped a beat. Damn, the man looked good. Having felt the hardness of his body already she knew he would look good shirtless, but nothing prepared her for the rippling muscles, the raw power of his body that seemed even more magnified out here where he was in his element. The view in front of her right now almost made up for the dust. Standing at Taxi's shoulder, where she could spy on Sam without being seen, she absently worked the brush in long strokes along Taxi's neck and tried to force thoughts of Sam from her mind.

Not thinking about Sam was easier said than done. Especially when he was so close, with so much of his powerful body on display. Her breasts tightened and ached with desire just looking at him. Peeking around Taxi's chest, she watched as Sam approached Trixie, the young horse she'd met just yesterday. The little mare that she'd started to bond with yesterday didn't much look like she wanted to go with Sam and when he tugged on the lead rope she planted all four feet firmly on the ground and baulked. Even from this distance, Marnie could see that Trixie was fighting him, and that endeared the horse to her even more. Anyone with enough guts to stand up to the brutish Sam was a winner in her book.

Trixie reared, striking out at Sam with her forelegs. Marnie gasped, both in fear and admiration. Instinctively, she took a few steps back from Taxi, just in case. He seemed calm and placid, but then so had Trixie, yesterday. Marnie eyed the gelding suspiciously, getting ready to run. Sam might be brave enough to hang onto the lead rope of a rearing horse, but she was not.

The muscles in Sam's back and shoulders rippled as he swung the long lead rope in a circle and the light sheen of sweat he'd worked up gleamed in the sun as he matched his movements to Trixie's, side-stepping, forward and back, an intricate dance. The heat in Marnie's breasts spread to her core.

Trixie looked the same way Marnie had felt last night—like she wanted to get away from Sam more than anything else, and she would fight with everything she had before she would submit to his will. Her ears were back, her body was tense, her nostrils were flared as she snorted, prancing, jumping on the spot. Even with Marnie's extremely limited knowledge of horses, it was obvious that Trixie was giving Sam a hard time. Just like Marnie herself, she wasn't going to do as she was told. Marnie felt an instant rapport with the horse—kindred spirits. Both out to give Sam hell.

Marnie watched, with bated breath, the battle play out between man and horse, with neither willing to give an inch. Although she had no idea what it was Sam was trying to make Trixie do, it was pretty obvious that Trixie had no intention of doing it. She was cheering Trixie on inside her head, wanting the little horse to win if for no other reason than to prove to Sam that he couldn't always be the boss.

They were front-on to her now. Trixie reared again, her forelegs striking out at the height of Sam's head, one on each side of him. Marnie's heart pounded. The horse was going to kill him! Her hooves touched the ground for just a second before she reared again, and still, Sam didn't back down.

Marnie was surprised by Sam's patience. She'd supposed he would have lost it and whipped the horse by now, just as he'd whipped her last night, but he didn't. Every movement he made was controlled, exact. She couldn't see his face, but from the back, it didn't look like he was even close to losing his temper. The heat in her core spread even further, making her pussy clench with desire. The more she watched Sam's skilled, powerful body, the more she wanted him.

Eventually, Trixie moved away from him, just a couple of steps, and Sam's whole body language changed. Even from here, she could see the difference in his body, the relaxed demeanour, the un-flexed muscles. That same soothing tone of approval she'd heard in his voice earlier wafted over to her on the gentle breeze. What would she have to do to get him to speak to her the same way?

Marnie jumped as Taxi's velvety lips settled on the back of her neck, shocking her out of her trance. Gripping the brush properly, she picked up where she'd inadvertently left off, slowly ridding Taxi of all his mud.

Trixie looked relaxed now, as Sam ran his hands over her body, throwing the end of the rope up and over her back, speaking to her in a voice so low that Marnie couldn't hear it. Inside, Marnie was a turmoil of emotions. She'd been rooting for Trixie, so badly wanting the horse to win. But at the same time, seeing those hooves so close to Sam's head had been terrifying. She'd wanted Trixie to win, but she hadn't wanted Sam to get hurt in the process. She felt oddly deflated, now that it was over. The fight had been won; Sam had bent another creature to his will.

CHAPTER SIX

Marnie wasn't sure she liked horses. They were nice when they were calm, but seeing what Trixie had nearly done to Sam had been frightening. Horses had big bone fists on their feet, and they were much, much bigger than people. Suddenly the whole situation seemed more overwhelming than ever. She was stuck with giant animals that liked to punch and a man who liked to spank. She didn't know which beast was worst.

"He's still dirty," Sam frowned as he came over. He was done with Trixie and now he was back dealing with her and her inept horse work.

"I didn't want him to do that thing…"

"What thing?"

"The…" She pawed at the air with her hands like hooves. "I don't want him to punch me with his feet."

Sam smirked. "Taxi isn't really a feet punching kind of guy, but it is good to be cautious around horses. Here, watch."

She stood back while Sam took over, brushing the dirt from Taxi's coat with strong strokes. It took him about two minutes to do the job she'd been attempting for the better part of an hour. When he was done, he checked his watch.

"Well, I was hoping to get you on your first ride today, but I reckon you need something to wear first. Let's go shopping."

"Where?"

"Culverden."

The name was vaguely familiar. A little town on the state highway. She'd passed through it a few times on girl's trips up to Hanmer Springs. It wasn't exactly a bustling metropolis. Marnie couldn't imagine what kind of clothes they'd have there.

Sam put Taxi and Trixie back in their paddock, then told her to follow him. She got into the dirty truck and they set off. Sitting wasn't entirely comfortable. Every jolt of the old suspension reminded her of what Sam had done to her and left her feeling shy. She looked out the window at the passing scenery and tried not to say anything.

"You alright?"

"Yeah."

"You're quiet."

She gave a little shrug.

He let the subject drop and put the radio on. Strains of music from the announcer proclaimed *70s, 80s, 90s and today* made their way out of the dusty grille near her knee.

"How far is it to Culverden?"

"'Bout an hour," he said.

An hour. Two hours there and back. All on a sore ass.

• • • • • • •

Marnie hadn't been herself lately. Not that he really knew her well enough to say exactly what she was like, but subdued wasn't one of the words he would have used yesterday. Since he'd spanked her before bed, she'd been quiet and even timid with him.

He didn't feel guilty about tanning her hide. She'd gone out of her way to deserve it. But he did feel bad if she didn't know how to take it and was afraid of him as a result.

"So," he said, intending on breaking the ice and getting to know her a little. "What do you like to do for fun?"

"Go out," Marnie said. "Or stay in."

So she liked to be indoors or outdoors. Well, that wasn't exactly a whole lot to go on.

They fell silent again. It was going to be a long drive.

Out of the corner of his eye, he could see her shifting uncomfortably on the seat.

"About last night…"

"Look, I know you're not interested in me, so you don't need to pretend," she said, tight-lipped. "I'm not going to throw myself at you again."

Sam sighed inwardly. He was not having this conversation over and over again. He'd explained very clearly what his reasons for wanting to refrain from sex were, and she was obviously smart enough to understand them.

By the time they got to Culverden it was almost lunchtime. Sam parked the ute outside the Culverden dairy and glanced over at Marnie.

"You want a pie?"

"Salad would be better."

"Yeah, nah, salad isn't really on the menu here. They have pies or hot chips or fried chicken."

"Chips then, please."

He got her some chips and some water. She stayed outside, next to the truck, her arms still folded over her chest, and when he brought her the food, she stayed there, pouting and nibbling while he sat in the truck and ate his pie and drank his L&P.

Shopping wasn't going to be fun, but it had to be done.

• • • • • • •

The store had a small range of women's clothing. There were jeans designed for riding, which would work well for her, and some Aertex shirts that would be perfect for the farm. Sam also intended on making sure she got some low-heeled riding boots that would fit, and some decent length socks too. She basically needed everything besides underwear.

"I don't wear bootleg jeans," she said, turning up her nose. "And I don't wear gingham."

"Well, they don't have a huge range, Marnie, and you need something long sleeved to keep the sun off. Try something on."

She did, reluctantly.

"I look stupid," she complained upon exiting the changing room.

She didn't look stupid. She looked adorable. The jeans were snug, encasing her sweet ass in a way that made his cock twitch. They were stretchy enough to ride in too.

"Okay, now boots."

She sat and sulked as she tried pull on boots, complaining that some were too tight and others were too loose until finally she said some would do. While Marnie made the assistant's life a nightmare, Sam had a look around the store. After what felt like an interminable length of time, there were three pairs of jeans and four shirts on the counter, along with socks and boots. Sam reached over Marnie and added an item to the pile—a riding crop.

"Don't you have enough of those already? There's a whole bin of them."

"Those are for the horses," he said. "This one's for you."

The checkout lady chuckled to herself, and added the cost to the bill. A couple hundred dollars later, he, the crop, and Marnie were out the door.

He'd thought she might be cheered up by the shopping trip, chicks usually loved spending other people's money, but Marnie didn't even say thanks. She just stamped her way back to the ute and got in, slamming the door behind her.

"What's wrong with you?" he asked as he got into the driver's side.

"You embarrassed me!" She growled the words, staring

straight ahead.

"How?"

"What you said at the counter."

"Oh, about the crop?"

"Yes, about the crop," she frowned. "That wasn't very nice. That lady laughed at me!"

"She wasn't laughing at you. She thought I was making a joke."

"No, she didn't."

"Well, so what?"

"So you embarrassed me!"

"Marnie, I'm about to really embarrass you if you don't stop acting like a spoiled little brat," he growled.

"Fire me."

"What?"

She looked at him fiercely. "I said fire me. Get rid of me."

"No."

"Asshole."

Sam gritted his teeth. He'd been about as patient as he could be with her, but nothing seemed to please Marnie. Apparently she'd decided to act like a brat until he slept with her. Fine.

He got the truck started and headed back toward home. Marnie sulked for a solid half-hour as they wound their way back up toward the farm. But what she didn't pick up on was the fact that they had turned down a lane before they got there and were heading up to a quiet little lookout only the locals really knew about. From there, the Canterbury plains were spread out below. It was beautiful, but Sam wasn't intending on taking in the view.

"What are we doing?"

He stopped the truck, got out, and walked around to Marnie's side. He wrenched the door open, unsnapped her seat belt, and pulled her out before turning her around and pushing her back down over the seat she'd just vacated. She spluttered and gasped, but he wasn't listening and she wasn't really saying anything anyway. Those short shorts betrayed her again as he grabbed the crop and started using it on the exposed part of her lower cheeks and the tops of her thighs, the leather tongue leaving splotches over the pale skin. The whip of the crop through the air was followed by a precious pink mark each and every time he brought it down, finding fresh skin to punish with every stroke.

Marnie screamed bloody murder, but that didn't stop him. Pouting and stamping and slamming things wasn't appropriate behaviour, and if that was what she had taken away from his punishment the night before, then obviously he hadn't done a very good job.

"You know why this is happening to you, little girl?"

"No!" Marnie shrieked.

"Because you're acting like a spoiled little brat. I told you last night. I'm in charge here, Marnie. You do as I say and you do it without pouting, understand?"

"You… Owww!"

She didn't have a chance to mouth off to him before he started working the crop over her ass again. This was the problem with spoiled animals of any kind, those who had learned bad lessons over time. The hardest horse to train was one who had already learned it could push people around. They took longer and required way harder working than any of the others. Marnie had obviously spent her life throwing her weight around, but she wasn't going to anymore. He'd work her little ass as long and hard as he needed to in order to bring her into line. He didn't care if she wanted it, or even if she understood. He wasn't dealing with the rational part of her. He was speaking directly to the animal inside this squirming little brat.

"Oww! Sam! I'm sorry!"

He stopped as soon as she made an apology.

"What are you sorry for?"

"I'm sorry for being a bitch," she said, using a word he personally wouldn't have chosen, but which fit.

Sam ran the tip of the crop over her hot cheeks, stroking

it gently between her thighs too. "You know better, don't you?" He made his voice deep and calm.

"…yes…" The admission came as a squeak.

"I don't know who made you think that being angry would get you what you wanted, but whoever it was didn't do you any favours. I don't respond to sulking or pouting, little girl. If you're upset, you talk to me. I might not be able to fix what's bothering you, but it will save you this."

• • • • • • •

Marnie wanted to be mad, but she'd known the minute she'd gone slamming out of the shop she'd pushed him too far. It had just been too hard to climb down off her high horse and apologize. She was so confused and so sore. The crop stung like hell, but his large hand spread between her shoulder blades felt good, as did having her legs spread for him again.

Was she losing her mind for this man? All she wanted was him inside her and it was driving her mad not being able to have him. She lifted her ass up a little, feeling the crop trail down and then up between her thighs.

Sam ran the leather over her denim-clad pussy, then gave it the lightest flick. Marnie let out a soft moan and arched her back more.

"You need this, don't you," Sam said in that rough but gentle voice.

"Yes…" she breathed the word as he tapped the crop against her sex again, working the tip up and down her crotch, whipping her protected slit with firmer and firmer swats until she moaned with desire.

"You're in heat," he growled, putting the crop to the side and replacing it with his hand. He cupped her pussy and squeezed. "I can smell you, Marnie. You need to be fucked, but I can't do that. Not now. We're going to have to find another way to get you off, my girl."

"Why?"

"Because I'm taking my time with you, remember?" He spanked her pussy lightly and she moaned again.

Then she felt his fingers working inside her shorts, his thick digits finding her wet slit. She was more than ready for him. She wanted his cock, but what she got were two fingers pushing inside her, his other hand yanking at her shorts, spreading her ass cheeks as he started to finger her right there in the car park.

"Oh, fuck, Sam…" She gripped the car seat as he pounded her pussy with his fingers, working them in and out of that tight wet hole. She spread her legs as wide as she could, just faintly aware that she was making a spectacle of herself in a public place. Sam made her mad with arousal. She didn't care about anything besides him.

"I want to fuck you, Marnie…" There was thick lust in his voice. "Fuck…"

Was he going to do it? Was he going to give in? She hoped so. When he pulled his fingers from her pussy, she thoroughly expected them to be replaced with his cock. But instead he pulled her from the car and pushed her to her knees in the dirt, his hands working at his fly to free his cock. He grabbed her by the hair and pulled her mouth onto his dick, taking her roughly.

"Touch yourself," he ordered. "Make your pussy come."

He worked her head back and forth along his shaft, using her lips as she stuffed her hand down the front of her shorts and played with her clit. Sam's cock was so fucking swollen and hard inside her mouth, pounding deep and long. She was going to come. She knew it. She couldn't help it. And so was he. He held her head still with both hands and thrust in and out until he let out a shout of triumph and release, his seed spilling over her tongue as she rubbed her slippery wet clit to the best orgasm she'd ever given herself, drinking his cum down eagerly.

"Good girl," he said, holding her in place, looking down at her with those brilliant blue eyes. "Such a fucking good girl."

• • • • • • •

Marnie was silent for the rest of the way home. It wasn't an uncomfortable silence as it had been before, but more of a peaceful one. Sam glanced across to see a satisfied, smug smile plastered across his quiet passenger's face. She was happy then; good. He missed her being happy. Not that he'd known her for very long, but he liked to think she hadn't been miserable for her entire time with him. He didn't consider himself to be a cruel man, and having a permanently unhappy woman for company didn't make him feel good at all.

Sam intended to teach her to ride when they got back to the farm. She could put on those new clothes he'd just spent a small fortune on and he'd take her down the river, where he led the treks sometimes. She'd like it down there. He'd been meaning to take her to the waterfall on the bike yesterday, but they'd got... *distracted*. A small chuckle escaped his lips. It had been a nice distracted, very nice actually, but still, he hadn't shown her the river or the waterfall like he'd intended.

When they got back, he would put her up on Taxi, putt around the paddock together a couple of times, then they'd set off. Sam was a firm believer that the best way to learn to ride was just to get on and ride; to face the fear and do it anyway. As long as the mount was safe and steady, it was the best method there was, in his opinion. And Taxi was nothing if not safe and steady. If Marnie was going to be any help to him at all this season, he would have to get her confident around horses, and soon. Maybe having her watch him work with Trixie had been a bad idea. He known at the time it could have gone either way with the little mare—sometimes she behaved, sometimes she didn't, much like Marnie herself. But unlike Marnie, Trixie's size and strength made her dangerous. But just like Marnie, Trixie was sweet underneath it all, and he was as drawn to

94

the horse as he was to the girl.

He didn't do his usual drifty sliding around the corner as he liked to do, out of respect to Marnie, who was still sitting there in silence looking pretty pleased with herself. He should have slowed down and changed down a gear before clattering over the cattle grid though—the suspension on the old ute wasn't the best and they bounced, Marnie's head nearly hit the ceiling of the cab, and she yelped as her bottom came back into contact with the seat.

"Sorry," he mumbled. "Old habits die hard."

"'s okay."

Shocked to his core, Sam nearly ran off the narrow strip of gravel that passed as a road. He'd been expecting her to unleash a tirade of vitriol, or for her at least to utter a small complaint. Her simple acceptance of his apology was a complete turnaround. Good, but unexpected. Had their relationship finally turned a corner? Was she possibly going to treat him as a friend, rather than the enemy, now?

Sam slowed down for the corrugations up ahead. They really needed to get the grader through again before they were inundated with trekkers—he'd have to get Aunt Magda onto it. The little city cars that so many of them arrived in would struggle over these bumps and dips in the road.

"Once we get back you can go and put your new clothes on, then we'll go riding," Sam announced.

"I don't want to go riding." Marnie pouted. "I hurt."

Sam sighed. He'd been so hopeful that Marnie's attitude had changed for the better, but it didn't appear that it had, after all. He took out his frustration on the steering wheel, tightening his grip around it until his knuckles went white. "You're here to work, remember? Part of that work will be riding, leading treks," he said through gritted teeth. "There isn't a lot of time for you to learn. And to be honest, if you're not used to riding, your backside is going to hurt after being in the saddle for a while anyway. Even if you hadn't been a naughty girl and gotten yourself spanked. You'll be fine."

Marnie didn't say a word, but when Sam looked across at her, the smile had gone from her face and had been replaced with a look of apprehension, almost fear. Stretching out a hand, he rested his palm lightly on her thigh, his fingers splayed across her warm, bare skin.

"You'll be fine, I promise," he murmured. "I teach people to ride every day. Taxi will look after you. He's a gentleman."

"Not like you, then."

Sam chuckled. "No. Not like me."

• • • • • • •

In the privacy of her bedroom, without Sam around, Marnie spread her new clothes out on her bed and fingered the fabric. They were totally not her style, but they were actually quite nice, and made her feel a little bit like she belonged. Maybe if she looked the part, it would be easier to act the part, too.

She regretted the ungrateful way she'd acted at the shop. It was nice of Sam to buy her these clothes, and she hadn't even thanked him. Come to think of it, she hadn't thanked him for the food he'd bought her, either. Or for anything else he'd done for her. A flash of guilt shot through her. Was it true, those words he'd said to her as he'd whipped her ass with that evil crop? Was she a spoiled little brat? She wasn't, really, although she had to admit she had been acting like one. A little bit, anyway. She should probably try to be a bit nicer to him. Especially if he was going to use that crop on her every time she wasn't.

The fabric of her shorts scraped against the welts the crop had left on the back of her thighs and she winced as she slid them down. Turning, she checked out her rear end in the mirror. Damn, the man was a brute! Her entire bottom was pinkish, slightly bruised looking, and crisscrossed with darker red lines where he'd plied the riding crop. *You deserved it, you were a bitch,* her subconscious reminded her. Reaching back, she touched the nastiest-looking welt gently. It stung. She couldn't believe she'd sucked him off. Not when he'd just done that to her. Even if her orgasm had been great, she should hate him. She hissed in pain as the brand new pair of jeans she was pulling on rubbed her tender bottom roughly. She should definitely hate him. She should, but she didn't.

Once they were on, the jeans were comfortable enough. They fit her so snugly they felt like they'd been made just for her. And although the shirt was totally not her, it, too, was comfortable enough. The darts in the side hugged her small waist and if she thrust her chest out, the buttons gaped slightly across her cleavage. Not exactly the sexy look she was used to, but it would do.

She felt Sam's eyes on her the second she walked out the door. He didn't say anything, but she knew he approved. His eyes followed her every move. Pausing, she met his lust-filled gaze then did a little twirl.

"You like?" She smiled. "Thank you. They fit perfectly."

Sam's grin lit up his entire face, making her all melty inside. She'd been attracted to him right from the start, but he was definitely far sexier smiling than scolding. He didn't answer her question, but by the look on his face, it was clear he was pleased.

Tingles shot up her spine when he laid his big hand in the centre of her back to guide her out to the barn. The last time he'd put his hand on her back like that had been to bend her over the ute seat to punish her. *I'm in charge here, Marnie* rang in her ears. He wasn't whipping her this time, but the gentle pressure of his huge hand nestled in her back reminded her that he truly was in charge, of everything.

Before they got to the barn, Sam stopped at a metal gate leading into another paddock and whistled. In just a few seconds, a huge chestnut beast came galloping toward them. He was ginormous, towering over her and nearly dwarfing Sam. Marnie took a step back.

"It's okay, Marnie, just relax. This is Fred. He won't hurt

you, he's gentle as a lamb." Sam's deep voice rumbled through her, soothing her, but she couldn't relax. Not properly. Not when there was an animal the size of a small elephant standing right there, ready to run her over.

"But he's so big," she breathed.

"Yep," Sam confirmed. "Seventeen hands. He's a big boy, but gentle. Here, hold out your hand."

Tentatively, she stretched out her hand, her fingers tightly closed, and shut her eyes, only to open them again when Sam's fingers enclosed around her wrist. With his other hand, he prised open her fingers and placed a piece of apple on her palm.

"Hold your hand flat, like this."

She copied his example, and he helped her, his big hand underneath hers steadying her shaking wrist. Tingles went up her spine as Fred lowered his head and gently took her offering, his lips tickling her palm. He nickered softly, perhaps thanking her, as Sam's strong arm went around her waist, pulling her in close to him.

"He won't hurt you, I promise."

They walked like that the rest of the way to the barn, Marnie tucked up against Sam's side, with the big horse following along so close behind Marnie could feel his warm breath on the back of her neck. She kept waiting for him to run her over, or to rear up and punch out with his feet like Trixie had done, but it never happened. And Sam didn't seem concerned at all to have a horse clip-clopping along behind them and gradually, she relaxed. Maybe Sam was right after all. Maybe Fred was safe enough.

Fred went straight to the hay net tied to the fence railing that Taxi had been nibbling on earlier, and it didn't take long for Sam to put a halter on him and tie him up. Taxi came up to the fence all by himself, and it didn't take long for Sam to get him tied up, either. Marnie watched, nervous. She wasn't too sure about this. Those horses were big, and it was a long way to fall... maybe she should refuse to get on.

Sam didn't tell her to brush Taxi this time. He seemed

content to do all the work himself while she stood back and watched, growing more and more uncertain. Sam moved between the two horses easily, confidently, seemingly unafraid. He brushed them, picked out their feet, pressed metal bits into their mouths and latched up bridles. Neither horse moved. Fred was tall, as tall as Sam himself, but Sam threw the saddle on his back effortlessly and pulled the girth tight, his biceps bulging through his shirt as he did so.

"Get your helmet."

Marnie froze. This was getting far too real, now. Getting on the back of the motorbike had been scary enough, and then there had been Sam to hang onto, and it was far closer to the ground. Now, unless she was mistaken, Sam intended for her to sit on the horse by herself, and it was much higher up, and it had a mind of its own. How was she supposed to make it go? More important, how was she supposed to make it stop?

She didn't want to get her helmet. She was quite happy right where she was, with both feet planted firmly on the ground. She had no desire whatsoever to climb up into a wobbly saddle, to be rocked around on a horse that may or may not buck her off and send her flying into the dirt. Why did she have to learn to ride, anyway? Coming here was a bad idea. A very bad idea.

"I'm... are you sure... I'm scared."

In two strides, Sam was in front of her. He grabbed her by both shoulders and shook her gently, but his eyes were kind. His eyes were perhaps the kindest she'd ever seen them, as he held her firmly.

"Marnie, it will be fine. You'll enjoy it, I promise you. Once you're up there, it's the best thing in the world. There's nothing else like it."

She looked at the ground. She couldn't meet his eyes. She knew she was disappointing him, but she was afraid. The horses were so big and...

"Look at me." With one hand, he tilted her chin up to look at him, and with the other, he brushed a stray lock of hair back off her forehead. Slowly, she met his gaze.

"I'm going to be right there beside you all the way. You're not going to come to any harm. Taxi does this all the time—he teaches people to ride. He's good at it." He stared at her harder, and a shiver went down her spine.

"Do you trust me?"

"I trust you." The words slipped out before she could stop them, but as she thought about it, she realized they were true. He'd scolded her, spanked her, fucked her, embarrassed her, whipped her, and used her body for his own carnal pleasure. He'd also fed her, taken her shopping, came charging to her rescue when she screamed, and cuddled her close when she cried. Yes, she trusted him. He was the first person she'd trusted in a long time.

He smiled, his approval turning her insides to mush.

"So relax. I've got you."

Sam helped her fasten her helmet, then he led her, with her heart pounding harder at every step, toward Taxi. She almost couldn't breathe, she was so scared. But Sam took her hand and placed it way up high on Taxi's neck, just below his ear. Holding her wrist gently, Sam smoothed her hand all the way down Taxi's sleek neck, then closed her fingers around a handful of his mane, just in front of the saddle. Keeping his body close to hers, he lifted her left leg and guided her foot into the stirrup.

"One, two, three, jump!"

She only jumped a little bit, too terrified to do it properly, but Sam boosted her at the same time, and his strong hands around her waist settled her into the saddle. He kept his hands there, holding her, while she felt her muscles adjust to the thickness of the horse beneath her. Her bottom throbbed, but she was too terrified to feel much in the way of pain, really. All she could think about, all she could feel, was fear. It washed over her in waves, crashing down on top of her, threatening to topple her, but Sam's strong hands steadied her, waiting for her to find her balance. Taxi didn't move.

Now that she knew she wasn't going to fall off just yet, Marnie let out the breath she hadn't realized she'd been holding. The saddle was starting to feel secure now, a bit like a chair, and Sam must have known this because he handed her the reins, sliding her fingers along the leather, closing them into position.

"Okay?"

To answer him, Marnie had to look down. It was a good feeling, being above Sam, even if he was technically still in charge. She smiled.

"We're going to walk now. Do you trust me?"

"Yes," she breathed.

• • • • • • •

Sam had half expected her to say 'no.' To hear the word 'yes' from her lips both surprised and pleased him. Obviously, he'd done something right.

The first step Taxi took nearly unseated her and he got ready to grab her, but after a few seconds she got the hang of it, relaxing into the saddle, letting her hips rock with the motion of the horse. She was a natural. He thought she would be, she had a good sense of balance; he'd discovered that when she'd been on the back of the bike. And the way she'd started to bond with Trixie yesterday told him that she would pick up riding pretty quickly. She wiggled in the saddle and winced slightly and he felt a momentary stab of guilt. He'd been pretty hard on her. Had he been too hard? But the wince disappeared and a proud smile spread across her face instead.

"I'm doing it! Sam, I'm doing it! I'm riding a horse!"

Sam couldn't help but chuckle. Her enthusiasm was infectious.

"And a fine job you're doing of it, too, little girl. You ready to learn the controls?"

Being a trekking horse, Taxi was fairly used to being booted and hauled about every which way by inexperienced riders, and had long since learned not to react. Sam never let the riders be rough, but still, Taxi was used to fairly obvious directions, and didn't follow subtle commands anymore. He could teach her the intricacies of subtle body language cues later, if she wanted to learn, but Taxi wasn't the type of horse to learn them on.

Tingles of passion shot up Sam's arms when he ran his hand down Marnie's calf, adjusting her foot in the stirrup and showing her how to press her leg against Taxi to make him move where she wanted him to go. His palms nearly burst into flames from the electricity sparking between them as he enclosed her fingers in his, helped her gather up the reins, and showed her how to steer and stop.

"Good girl." He murmured it almost under his breath but she heard, and he couldn't help but notice the way her face lit up at the unexpected praise.

"Okay, ride a couple of times around the pen here, then we'll go for a proper ride, once you're comfortable." Stepping back, Sam gave her full control of the gelding, but watched her carefully for signs of panic. If she was going to freak out at all, she would do it now. But the smile never left her face as Taxi ambled slowly around the pen, and even though she clearly winced several times, it was obvious she was enjoying herself.

He couldn't take his eyes off her. She was gorgeous when she smiled, and although her new red checked shirt clashed horribly with her pink helmet, she looked adorable on top of Taxi. He wanted to haul her out of the saddle and rip off her clothes... *Don't!* he commanded himself harshly. *Your cock has caused enough trouble.*

"Straighten up." His voice was husky with arousal and even to his own ears, sounded gruff.

"Huh?" She sounded confused, but looked hurt, probably at his gruffness. She obviously responded better to praise than what she perceived as correction. He made a mental note of that for the future. It would be much easier to teach her what he needed her to know, if he knew the way she worked.

"You're tilted forward," he said, gentling his voice.

"That's cos my butt hurts." Her voice had a distinct *duh!* snark to it, and she accompanied it with a filthy look no doubt meant to put him in his place, but he let it ride.

"Well, riding like that is going to do really nasty things to your lady parts. Rubbing against the saddle like that is going to give you chafing like you wouldn't believe. It won't be pleasant tomorrow, for you. So straighten your back, like this." Sparks sizzled between them as he touched her, one hand on her belly, the other on her back, pressing her into position. Electricity zinged up his arm as he prodded her with his fingers, straightening her body, his thumb hovering just above her crotch. All he had to do was reach down and... *stop!*

He inhaled long, slow. "That's better. Good girl."

Leaving them to it for a moment, he snuck out of the pen to get Fred. He couldn't keep watching her, not when every fibre of his being was aching for her. It was either pull her off the horse and ravish her here in the dust, or do his best to distract himself. He chose the latter. It wouldn't be comfortable riding with a raging erection, but he didn't have much choice.

• • • • • • •

Marnie had never seen Sam ride. But he looked every bit as sexy in the saddle as he did on the ground. Being up so high emphasized his wide shoulders and narrow hips, and the muscles in his thighs were outlined as he wrapped his legs around his horse. The butterflies in her tummy fluttered madly and sent heat straight to her core. Ignoring Sam's instructions about her riding posture, she tilted her pelvis forward again so her clit rubbed against the saddle and sighed softly.

She felt so naughty, doing exactly what Sam had told her not to do. But the incredible sensations ricocheting through her body right now would make any painful chafing tomorrow worth it. Taxi ambled along slowly behind Sam because the rough trail was too narrow for anything other than single file, but every now and then Sam would turn in his saddle and look back at her, making sure she was doing okay. The graceful way he moved his hips so just his upper body turned did delightful things to her insides. She squirmed a bit more in the saddle, clutched the reins a bit tighter in her fingers, and worked her clit furiously against the leather, moving in time with Taxi's steps, each rocking motion taking her closer and closer to the edge. Her breasts tightened, aching, to match the throbbing in her pussy. Throbbing that changed and turned and tingled with each step.

Tangling her fingers in Taxi's mane, she gave a small cry as she shattered, holding on for dear life as wave after wave of intense pleasure washed over her.

Sam turned in the saddle. "Are you okay?"

• • • • • • •

"Y… yes," Marnie stammered.

From her rapid breathing, flushed face, dilated pupils and weird voice it wasn't hard to guess what Marnie had been doing. The naughty little minx! Sam hid his smile. She'd gotten herself off on the bike, too. Riding things clearly agreed with her. He needed to teach her a lesson.

The stubble on his jaw scratched his fingers as he rubbed his chin, deep in thought. He couldn't bring himself to spank her again, not after whipping her so soundly on the way home, but at the same time, he couldn't let her go unpunished. Still, there was more than one way to skin a cat. An evil grin slowly spread across his face as the answer came to him.

"You're doing well, little girl," Sam declared. "Come on, let's trot."

He waited until the trail widened up ahead and there was

room for them to ride side by side before he urged Fred into a trot. He was fairly sure that trotting wouldn't make Marnie fall off, but he wanted to be sure. He wanted to punish her, but he didn't actually want her falling and hurting herself. If she wasn't used to coming off horses, the ground was a long way down.

"You ready? Squeeze your legs tighter around him, click to him with your tongue, that's it. Good girl."

Sam sat easily in the saddle to the two-beat gait, but beside him, Marnie was bouncing around, which was exactly what he'd intended to happen. She yelped every time her bruised rear contacted the saddle. He'd forgotten just how bouncy Taxi's trot was; Fred's gait was far smoother.

Marnie's yelps grew more and more desperate. A quick glance across at her face told Sam what he already knew—this was torture for her. She looked close to tears, and totally miserable. It was clear she'd been punished enough.

"You've got the hang of that really well," he said encouragingly. "I'll teach you how to rise to the trot now, you'll find it much more comfortable. You ready?"

Marnie nodded miserably.

He demonstrated on Fred, using his thighs to propel him upward in the saddle with the movement of Fred's legs. It was simply a matter of finding the beat, and rising up with it. A bit like dancing, really. That was something else he'd have to do with Marnie, spin her around on a dance floor. He had a feeling she'd be a natural at that, too.

"See? Now you try. Up, down. Up, down. Up, down." He guided her, watching Taxi's legs so he could tell her to move at the right time, but he needn't have bothered; she picked up the rhythm really quickly.

Sam watched the relief wash over her face. Her bottom was still impacting the saddle, but in a more controlled way instead of just bouncing. Already, she held the reins lightly, along with a handful of mane, and he was pleased to see she kept her heels down in the stirrups, just as he'd taught her. He smiled broadly. Maybe Marnie would be far more useful to him than he'd first thought.

After a few minutes of trotting, Sam brought Fred back to a walk. Taxi followed suit. For her first ride, Marnie had probably done enough. He didn't want her so sore tomorrow that she was put off riding completely, not when she was showing so much potential.

Edging Fred up to a gate, he leaned down and opened it, ushering Marnie and Taxi through.

"Just over that rise there is the barn," he said softly. "You go on ahead, I'll catch up."

• • • • • • •

Riding was much more fun than Marnie had imagined it would be, but it hurt more too, especially on a sore ass. Sam had known the state of her rear when he made them go faster. He'd wanted her bottom to hurt. Sadistic bastard. She'd been on the verge of bursting into tears until he finally let her slow down.

She should hate him, but now that the pressure was off and the pain of trotting had receded, Marnie found herself with a secret little smile on her face. She kind of liked that side of Sam. There weren't many men who could put up with her when she was at her worst. Sam didn't just meet her where she was, he outpaced her, raised the bar, and made her realize that she really didn't want to mess with him.

Taxi plodded back toward the barn, almost as if he was automated. He knew the way better than she did so Marnie sat there, more a passenger than a rider, and looked out over the countryside. The sun was starting to get low in the sky and red flares were starting to break over the horizon, casting a red glow over the land. It was stunning out here. There was no denying it. She had gotten lucky in being able to come out here. There were still so many people back in Christchurch dealing with ongoing aftershocks and endless insurance issues. None of those mundane practical concerns seemed to touch this place. It was almost as if the land itself were enchanted, a place apart from the modern world with all its nonsense.

Glancing over her shoulder, she saw Sam bringing up the rear. God, he was so impossibly handsome with his hard body framed in silhouette against the sky. Her movement in the saddle pushed her hips forward. She noticed that she could feel a tingle between her thighs, but unlike usual it was not an entirely pleasant one. Maybe she should have listened to him when he told her not to ride with her hips tilted forward, but it was too late now.

Taxi parked himself next to the tie point and Marnie swung her feet out of the stirrups and slid off on his left slide. As she dismounted, she felt a sharp pinching sensation between her thighs. Oh, yeah. There was chafing. And it was much worse walking than it had been riding.

"Ow," she mumbled as she walked bow-legged around Taxi, loosening the buckles that held the saddle on.

"I tried to tell you, little girl," Sam said as he rode up. "You're going to be sore. Be careful when you get in the shower tonight. It's going to sting like hell."

"How do you know? Does riding hurt your vagina too?"

Whap!

Sam belted his crop across her ass. He didn't even have to leave Fred to do it, and the extra distance gave that devilish leather tongue even more sting than usual.

Taxi flicked an ear as Marnie gasped in pain and clenched at her ass. "Ow! Sam!"

He smirked down at her. "Feel like being a smart mouth again?"

"No," she grumbled.

"Good," he said. "Unsaddle Taxi and then give him a good brush down."

Horses were a lot of work, but there was a certain satisfaction in removing the saddle and then taking a rubber comb and working it over the area where the saddle had been rubbing. The hair beneath was a little sweaty from where Taxi had been working, and he seemed to appreciate her efforts to make him feel better, nickering in a contented way. There was plenty of discomfort out here, earned and unearned, but Marnie reckoned she could get used to this.

CHAPTER SEVEN

A week passed. Marnie learned how to ride. She wasn't perfect at it, but she got to the point that she could rise to a trot and even stand up in the stirrups so her butt didn't meet the saddle at all. Sam said he'd teach her to canter soon, but he wanted her to get comfortable at the walk and the trot first and she was okay with that. There was no rush to go faster, and she didn't think Taxi would probably go much faster anyway. Getting him to trot at all was sometimes a bit of a mission, and he'd slow down as soon as he was allowed to. He was a lazy old man in every sense of the word.

Sam kept his word in so far as staying away from her in an erotic sense, but that was okay because about two days after her first ride, she got her period. No wonder she'd been so snippy and short with Sam from the beginning. Her PMS was pretty bad sometimes, and since the quakes her periods had been hard to predict.

Riding seemed to help the cramps though, especially the gentle strolls through the countryside. Sam took her on one almost every afternoon or early evening, to get a sense of the terrain they'd be working customers over once the season kicked into full swing. They'd had a few visitors already, small groups of two to four people who had gone out with Sam after Marnie helped saddle them all up.

Sometimes people asked her questions about horses. She didn't even pretend to know, just directed all the questions to Sam by repeating them. He seemed to be okay with that, and she learned a lot from listening to the answers he gave. She was getting used to the horses too. They all had their own personalities, likes and dislikes. Most all of them liked to be brushed and loved on, and they all liked apples and carrots. Marnie was even getting used to picking out their hooves and clearing out stalls. It was dirty work, but it wasn't as humiliating as it had seemed at first. It needed to be done to look after the horses, and she liked looking after them. It was nice to have something to care about. Since the quakes she'd mostly worried about herself.

One afternoon Sam was out with a small group and Marnie was picking up around the stables, wheeling a barrow of manure to the pile out the back. As she worked, Trixie came prancing down the fence line, her head high, her tail raised. Sam hadn't taken her out on the ride either.

"I know, we've been left behind," she said to the horse. "It's not fair, is it."

Trixie whinnied and shook her head, watching curiously as Marnie upended the barrow and sent the manure into the stash. She wasn't sure what it was used for. Some kind of fertilizer, maybe. When she was done she went over and said hello to Trixie. The filly liked to have her nose rubbed and Marnie did that until Trixie started nibbling on her. Every chance Trixie got to misbehave, she took.

"Okay, that's enough. I got more stalls to do," Marnie said, returning with the barrow. Her legs were starting to tire from standing up and working for so long. She needed to sit down. There weren't a lot of places to do that. The barn was a work area, not designed for human comfort. There was one place where she knew there had to be a chair though—Sam's office.

It was a little room at the back of the barn, not much more than a boarded-up stall, but it seemed to do the trick.

She'd been in there once or twice to handle client paperwork and she knew there was a chair in there. She could sneak away for a few minutes and take a load off her feet, she figured. Sam wouldn't even know.

Smiling to herself, Marnie returned the wheelbarrow to its usual place and went into Sam's office. An old but comfy leather chair awaited her and she sank into it with a sigh of relief. All the horse trek work was crazy physical, and the early mornings didn't really help either.

She sat back and closed her eyes for a bit, just enjoying the rest. Oh, yeah. This was nice. She should do this more often. She half-opened her eyes and looked around the office casually, just taking things in. As she did, something caught her eye. A piece of paper sitting on Sam's desk, marked with red lettering.

Marnie instantly knew she shouldn't look at it. That would be snooping. It wasn't any of her business. But letters in that typeface with that angry red stamp above them just demanded to be read. She sat up a little taller in the chair and squinted her eyes to look at the letter. The logo on the upper right hand corner told her that it was from the bank, but she couldn't read the writing until she got up out of the chair and looked at it a little closer, glancing over it quickly.

There were some terse words and some very big numbers. She didn't have time to really take it all in, but the gist was clear. The business was deep in debt. No wonder there weren't any trained staff around. No wonder it was just her and Sam. No wonder her aunt had been so keen for her to help out. In an instant, everything fell into place.

Just as she got done reading, footsteps outside the office startled her. Was Sam back already? Usually trekkers made lots of noise when they returned, but maybe it wasn't as audible this far back in the barn. It was too late to get out of the office. Marnie froze, which was probably about the worst possible thing she could have done. She stared at the door, hoping that Sam wasn't coming into the office.

A second later his tall shadow fell over the door, and

then he was standing in front of her, a quizzical and unimpressed look on his face.

"What are you doing?"

"Uhm…"

He was blocking the doorway. There was no way out.

"I was just looking for a pen," she lied.

"A pen? Why?"

"So I could write my phone number down before I forgot it."

Stupid! She could have said anything. She could have said one of the clients asked for one. She could have said she wanted to write in her diary. Hell, she could have said she wanted to shove it up her butt and it would have been a more plausible explanation.

Both Sam's brows rose. "Little girl, that makes no sense. Why are you in here?"

"I was tired. My legs hurt, so I looked for somewhere to sit down…"

His eyes dropped to the piece of paper she had been looking at. "And you went through my financial records."

"It was right on top! I couldn't help seeing it. I'm sorry," she said earnestly. "Seriously, Sam. I am sorry. I'm sorry for looking and I'm sorry this place is in trouble. I had no idea."

"You still have no idea," he said gruffly, stepping forward to shove the bank's notice beneath a pile of other papers. "And it's not your concern. Get out of here, Marnie. This is off bounds to you."

The office wasn't a very big room. Getting out of there was going to mean going right past him and she really didn't want to risk his hand on her rear. He hadn't properly punished her since the day she'd acted up in Culverden. Part of her was glad for that—and part of her wasn't. Living in the same house as Sam, being woken up by him every day, working by his side, it was all a type of torture just barely mediated by the fact that she was sexually out of operation anyway.

"Out. Now."

"You're in the way."

He stood to the side and let her go past. Marnie put her head down and scurried by, putting her hands back over her butt to cover her rear. She heard him snort as she zipped by him, and before he could change his mind about punishing her, she escaped back to the farmhouse and took a shower. Magda would probably have tea ready soon. Usually Marnie would go down once she'd gotten changed and chat with Magda and tease Sam, but after getting cleaned up, she stayed in her room until Magda called and then she made her way downstairs for tea.

It was kind of uncomfortable. Sam was much quieter than he usually was. He avoided even looking at Marnie though he made plenty of polite conversation with Magda. With that sick feeling in her tummy that told her she was in trouble, Marnie ate quickly and moved to clear up the plates. Doing the dishes gave her a reason to escape the tension until she heard Aunty Magda make her goodbyes and head off to the little granny flat out back.

She and Sam had the house to themselves. Usually that was a good thing. Most nights they just watched TV until Sam sent her to bed—something that galled her, but wasn't worth arguing about. Tonight, she kind of wished Magda was around. She had a sense that the conversation about the bank statement wasn't over yet.

Sure enough, when she was done with the dishes Sam was waiting for her. As she went to leave the kitchen she found him sitting at the dinner table, drumming his fingers on the top. There was no way to go upstairs without going past him. Marnie dried her hands and tried to sidle past him anyway.

"Come here," he said, before she could get very far.

Marnie slid into the chair opposite him, avoiding his hard gaze. Sam was sexy when he was stern, but she really didn't want the lecture, or the punishment she knew she probably had coming.

"What you saw today," he said. "I want you to forget

about it, okay? It's not your problem. And it's not Aunty Magda's problem either. I took over this place and I'm going to turn it around."

Marnie nodded. "Well, I'm here to help, so…"

"You help by doing what you're told," he said firmly. "And staying out of my papers. I should spank you for getting into my office like that."

A flash of heat ran through Marnie and her ass broke into a sweat. She hadn't known it was possible for just one part of her anatomy to react, but Sam's habit of taking his displeasure out on her rear had quickly trained her bottom to expect the worst.

"I'm sorry," she said quickly, hoping to avoid punishment. "I know I shouldn't have looked. I was just going to sit down and rest my legs and I saw it and… I am sorry, Sam." She raised her eyes to him plaintively, hoping he'd forgive her.

"If I catch you in my office again, you'll pay, understand? I'm letting you off now because you've been really good the last week. Great with the clients, and with the horses, too. You're really coming along nicely, Marnie."

She couldn't help the broad smile that flashed over her features. "Really?"

"Yeah. Really. And it's getting you out of trouble this time, but it won't work again. Now get upstairs and get to bed."

"It's seven o'clock," she protested. "It's way too early to go to bed."

"Bed. Marnie. Now."

She opened her mouth to protest again, but thought better of it. If Sam wanted her out of his way, she'd give him his space. He was probably stressed as hell with everything going on, needing to do the books and stuff. She got up and scurried upstairs.

• • • • • •

Sam really wasn't happy that Marnie had found out his financial position. His aunt and uncle had unfortunately let the place go to ruin as they got older and their business had suffered over the last few years, but the bones were good. The horses were good. And tourism was picking up since the quakes, seeing as Christchurch wasn't exactly a huge draw in the broken city. If he had a good season, he could turn things around... that's what he was telling himself, anyway.

Objectively, the truth was things were bad and getting worse. The season was off to a slow start and without more hands to help, he couldn't run as many treks as he needed to. Marnie wasn't ready to take anybody out on her own, and probably wouldn't be this season. But that wasn't what he was most worried about now. The business was one thing. Marnie was another.

The expression on her face when he'd caught her had been guilty, but he'd seen something else in her eyes—pity. He really didn't want her pity. And he didn't want her thinking he couldn't take care of things. Like her.

The last week had been good. He'd managed to keep himself in check and give her some space. She'd settled down as well. They were starting to get to know one another properly. He'd been hoping that there would be a chance of a real relationship between them, one that wasn't entirely based on raw sexual attraction and poor impulse control. But now she knew he was in financial dire straits and if Sam knew anything about women, he knew that things were probably over between them.

Girls didn't want broke guys. Especially city girls like Marnie.

• • • • • • •

Sam was gruff the next morning. He barely looked at her, and spoke to her only when necessary. He barked orders at her, and looked like he'd barely slept a wink.

Ordinarily, she would snap at him or try to wind him up, but knowing what she now knew, she decided to cut him some slack. The amount of pressure he must be under would be immense.

If she was honest with herself, her choice to keep quiet and endure Sam's grumpiness was more about self-preservation than any act of consideration on her part. She knew his patience would be at an all-time low now that she knew about his financial situation and she definitely didn't want him taking his frustrations out on her butt. He did that enough without her provoking him.

As soon as the morning chores were done, he grouchily informed her that they were going for a ride up into the mountains, and she should start getting Taxi saddled up.

Marnie was proud of how quickly she'd learned to work with the horses. She was confident enough now to go out to the paddock and catch Taxi, put on his halter and bring him in, tie him up, fill his hay net, brush him down, pick out his feet, and saddle him up. All by herself. In just a week.

"You'll need a breastplate and crupper," he told her. "They're necessary pieces of equipment for high country riding; they'll stop the saddle slipping."

Marnie looked at him blankly. What the hell was he talking about? She'd thought she pretty much had the horsey lingo down pat, but those things sounded entirely foreign to her. She swallowed, discouraged. She'd thought she'd been doing so well, but reality had hit again, showing her just how much she still needed to learn to be useful here. How was she going to be of any help to Sam if she couldn't get her head around all the stuff there was to do?

Patiently, but without his usual energy and vigour, Sam showed her what a breastplate was, what it did, how to put it on, and explained why it was needed. He did the same with the crupper. Because the two new items were both integral pieces of equipment, it turned out that Sam saddled up Taxi all by himself, while she just stood there, watching. She felt entirely useless. The whole time Sam brushed Fred and saddled him up, Marnie waited by Taxi, pouting, totally crestfallen. She was useless. How was she going to help Sam save his business if she was too useless to help? More important, why did she even care?

They left the barn in a totally different direction than they normally did, heading to the mountains, along a trail she'd never noticed before. It led away from the buildings on an angle, into a native beech forest where the air was cooler and the tree canopy provided a natural, shady relief from the hot sun, alive with birdsong. The air was different in here, cleaner, crisper, earthier. She liked it. She'd never been the outdoorsy type before, and had much preferred the beach to the bush. But this was nice.

It didn't take too long for the track to start climbing. The incline was gradual at first but got steeper as they went on, winding between tree trunks, the trail so narrow in places that she had to press her knees hard in against Taxi's sides to avoid them being scraped on the rough bark. Birds took off suddenly, the sudden cacophony of wings and squawks made her jump, startled. In front of her, Fred stiffened, but Taxi didn't seem at all bothered, he just ambled along, stopping just before he crashed into Fred. Because she wasn't paying attention, the sudden stop jolted her body forward slightly, nearly unseating her, and she cried out in surprise.

Sam turned in his saddle. "You okay?"

Grasping Taxi's mane with both hands, Marnie nodded. "Yeah. Taxi just stopped suddenly and I wasn't ready, that's all." Just saying it, she felt stupid. How many people nearly fell off their horse at a walk? At this rate, she'd never be any good to Sam.

Just then, Sam got Fred moving again and they continued up the trail. She noticed the streaming sunshine at the same time she realized the trees were thinning out and giving way to rocky ground and the occasional tussock. Taxi rocked from side to side as he dodged boulders partially blocking the trail, and stepped over fallen sticks. She gripped his mane tightly in her fingers, clutching the reins with one hand. Once she got used to the different step and relaxed into the saddle, letting her hips rock with Taxi's movements, she really enjoyed the ride. They were pretty high up here and the view was spectacular. They were in the foothills of the Southern Alps and the mountain range was all she could see off to her right. But to her left, she could see right out to the sea at Kaikoura, across the rugged farmland, hills, trees, the river that meandered through the farm was directly below them… she was mesmerized. She pulled up briefly, just so she could stare. Wow! In every direction, the view took her breath away.

"Pretty cool, huh?"

She hadn't realized Sam had stopped as well, but of course he had; the lack of hoof beats behind him would have alerted him to the fact that Taxi had stopped moving.

"It's gorgeous," she breathed.

"Yep. One of my favourite places in the world. I can ride this track every day in the height of summer and never get tired of it." Sam's voice was proud, but there was a dejected demeanour about him as well. "Well, let's get going," he ordered, sounding much cheerier.

The trail levelled out a bit for a while, then started to climb steeply again, the rugged track bordered by jagged rocks and the uneven surface lined with tree roots. Again, Taxi's plodding motion turned bouncier as he carefully placed his feet.

Sam momentarily disappeared from sight as he rounded the sharp corner hidden by a cliff. Taxi sped up the slightest bit, breathing a bit more heavily now from the exertion. He kept so close to the cliff that her stirrup brushed against the rock.

"Uh, Sam?" she squeaked, panicking. To the right, there was a sheer drop-off, and to the left was a rock wall. The only way to go was up, on the narrow, steep, winding dirt track.

Sam twisted in his saddle to look back at her. "Just trust

your horse," he told her calmly. "He's done this plenty of times before and he's not going to fall off. Relax into the saddle, loosen your reins a bit, hold onto the mane instead. You're doing fine." There was an unmistakeable note of approval in his voice and Marnie swelled with pride. She'd been expecting derision, condescension, even a growling for being so frightened, so the encouragement was a nice surprise.

"This is challenging terrain we're on," Sam continued. "It's tricky riding. You're doing really well."

Sam looked so natural in the saddle. And up here, he seemed right at home, like he belonged. Looking down scared her, so she focused on Sam's back instead. Sweat dampened his shirt, making the thin cotton cling to his muscular frame. Even Fred's massive size failed to dwarf Sam's broad shoulders. She imagined running her hands across those wide shoulders, down his arms, and trailing her fingers downward while Sam wrapped those muscular arms around her. What would it be like to be riding with him, her chest pressed against his back, her pelvis rocking against his? She imagined him stopping the horses on a secluded part of the trail, under the shade of a big tree perhaps, and lifting her down, holding her in his arms, against his rock-hard body, and kissing her hungrily.

It seemed to take forever for the trail to widen again, level out, and move away from the dizzyingly close edge of the cliff. The rocky track opened up to flatter grassland dotted with clumps of mountain tussock. Once again, the scenery was spectacular.

Marnie relaxed. There was a companionable silence between them, the only sound the blowing of the horses and the rhythm of their hooves, along with the occasional squeak as the saddle shifted slightly. It was beautiful country up here. It felt like the wilderness. Now that she thought about it, compared to the city she'd grown up in and barely left, it *was* the wilderness. And now that she'd experienced it, she didn't want to ever leave.

"Thirsty?"

She took the drink bottle Sam held out to her and skulled gratefully. Water had never tasted so good. Somehow, the alpine air made it fresher and sweeter than it usually did, and she drank greedily.

They hopped off the horses and sat down in the grass, letting the horses graze for a bit. It was so peaceful up here and it was easy to believe that she and Sam were the only people in the world.

Marnie lay back in the grass, watching the clouds drift lazily across the sky. She hadn't felt this relaxed in... well, ever. She could easily imagine spending the summer up here, on horseback, sharing with Sam this place he clearly loved so much.

Riding back down didn't seem to take anywhere near as long as riding up. They took a different trail down, one that didn't wind along cliff faces with terrifying drops off to the side. Beech forest, mainly, opening out to grassy patches here and there, before going back into forest again. Most of it was fairly steep, but none of it made her feel like she was dicing with death.

Taxi plodded happily along behind Fred and Marnie relaxed, totally enjoying herself. Right now, it didn't matter that she was a complete novice. Right now, all that mattered was that she was having fun.

Her stomach rumbled. Must be lunchtime.

"We're not far from home now," Sam called.

Marnie felt herself blush, mortified. Sam had heard!

Sure enough, just over the slight rise, there was the barn in the distance. Taxi pricked his ears forward and picked up the pace, his sedate plod turning into a more enthusiastic, striding walk as the barn drew nearer. Marnie was surprised Taxi still had the energy to come so close to breaking into a run, after climbing those high country trails. He was obviously much fitter than he looked. If she had been the one doing the climbing, she would have died long ago. Hiking had never been one of her hobbies.

Sam jumped off Fred and tied him up. He glanced at his watch.

"Unsaddle both of them and give them a good brush down," he commanded. "I've got a call to make."

Marnie had never really done much with Fred before, but as she fiddled with all the buckles, trying to figure out how everything came off with all the unfamiliar equipment, he just stood there contentedly, unmoving, munching on the hay in his net. He was no different to Taxi, really, he was just bigger.

Sam took ages. Marnie had both horses unsaddled and brushed down and was absently kicking at a stone with her shoe when Sam finally appeared, his face grim. Without a word, he untied Fred and led him toward his paddock, motioning for Marnie to follow with Taxi.

A knot formed in the pit of her stomach. This was not good. Had Sam been talking to the bank? Was it bad? Was she going to have to leave? But she liked it here, dammit! She liked it, and she didn't want to leave. Not when she was finally getting used to it.

At first, when she'd been so far out of her comfort zone and terrified, she couldn't think of anything worse than working with horses, and the cantankerous man who was her boss. But now... now she couldn't think of anything worse than leaving her cantankerous boss behind and being forced back to the still-rocking city she once considered home but no longer wanted to live in.

She had to do something.

CHAPTER EIGHT

Marnie was sitting cross-legged on her bed when she heard heavy footsteps on the stairs. She had been expecting to hear from Sam sooner or later. It had been a week since their conversation in the kitchen, and she had ignored him when he said to leave the matter alone. Of course, she hadn't told him she was planning on doing something. There was no point arguing with Sam. Easier to go about her duties with the horses, keep her head down, and hope that when he figured out what she'd done, he wouldn't be too mad.

"Marnie!"

Sam boomed her name at the top of the stairs. He sounded pretty mad. She took a deep breath as he came striding into the room, a piece of paper in his hand, his teeth gritted at her. "Did you pay the mortgage?"

"What?" Marnie widened her eyes and spoke with a high lilting voice that she hoped would transmit innocence.

"Don't play dumb with me, little girl," he growled. "I just got a notification that we're up to date on our payments. Thirty thousand dollars was paid in two days ago!"

Most people would have been pleased to find their late payments made for them, but there was tension in every part of Sam's body, his hard frame locked with frustration. She shrank away from him a little and put an ingratiating smile on her face.

"Well, you bought me these jeans," she said, smoothing her hands over her pants. "I wanted to do something for you too."

"Since when do you have money?"

"Well. Uhm, I didn't, but my grandma's inheritance for me came through," she said. "And I talked to Magda and I said I'd been talking to you about investing and she gave me the account number, so I…"

"Spent your entire inheritance on late payments for a failing business?"

"It wasn't my entire inheritance," Marnie said with a little eye roll. "I've still got a couple grand left. And it's not a failing business. It was just in a little trouble. And now it's not. I fixed it!"

"It's not in a little trouble, Marnie. It's…" He shook his head, his teeth gritting as he emitted a little growl. "You should have talked to me first."

"I couldn't talk to you. You would have said no."

"Damn right I would have said no," he said, throwing the paper to the side. "I would have told you that you're my employee…"

"And that it's not my problem, and that I shouldn't worry, or help or do anything. That I should just sit here and eat your food and let you buy me stuff and not make any kind of a difference." She stood up, getting into his space. "Sam, I know what it's like to lose everything. I know that money is just the start. I know we're going to have to work hard. I know there's no guarantees, but I'm going to try anyway."

He looked down at her, his expression confused, and impressed, and stern. "Why would you care?"

"Because," she scowled at him. "I happen to like this place. I lost one home. I'm not losing another one."

"You like this place? Since when?"

"Shut up," she frowned. "I don't have to explain myself to you. I'm helping you and that's the end of it."

It wasn't a terribly good way to say what she was trying to say, and it didn't go down particularly well. Sam was already riled. He didn't need much more of a reason to take her to task.

Marnie let out a squeal as he grabbed her by the arm and yanked her over to the bed. Sitting down, he pulled her over his thighs and his hand met her jean-clad ass with a hard whack that made her yelp in pain. She wasn't surprised. Sam's answer for literally everything was to spank her.

"You don't tell me to shut up, Marnie," he growled. "You don't disrespect me. You don't damn well pay off my debts either. Little girl, you have overstepped your boundaries by a good long way."

"I wanted to help you!"

"You were helping me, by working with the horses and helping with the treks."

"It wasn't enough! You were never going to make that money up! You should be thanking me! At least you're not behind now!"

His hand came down more softly and rested on her ass.

"I know you meant to do something good, Marnie, but I didn't…" He took a deep breath. "I'm probably going to have to sell this place."

"What? No!"

"The house needs renovations that will cost thousands, and Magda took out a second mortgage a year or so before I took over. The payments on that are killing this business. Right now, property prices are as high as they've ever been. This place is worth far more sold to someone else than it is under my care."

No. This couldn't be happening. She wouldn't let it happen. Marnie started to squirm and wriggle. "Let me up, Sam!"

He released her and she sat up next to him, looking into his eyes with desperation as she felt her stomach twist. "You can't sell this place."

"I've already gotten an offer," he said. "There's a farming corporation looking to expand their intensive dairying business. They've offered enough to pay Magda out, cover the mortgage, and maybe leave enough over for me to pick up a five-acre lifestyle block somewhere."

Marnie shook her head. That would have been a happy ending for most people, but Sam didn't belong on a lifestyle block, a couple of pokey little paddocks surrounded by houses. He belonged out here, on the mountains and the plains.

"What about the horses?"

"I could keep a couple, but I'd probably have to sell most of them."

"No." Marnie shook her head. "That can't be what happens."

Sam put his hand on her shoulder. "When I sell, I'll make sure you're paid back."

"No!" Marnie yelled the word, her eyes filling with tears. "You're not selling this place. No."

"Marnie..."

"You're not even going to try to keep it? That's it?" She waved her hands in the air. "After everything we've been through?"

• • • • • • •

"I'm trying, Marnie," Sam said, attempting to reason with her. "I've been trying for a long time, but at some point, practical decisions have to be made."

"Fuck practical decisions!"

Part of Sam agreed with Marnie, but he was still mad as hell at her. She shouldn't be throwing her money away on this place. He hadn't asked for it. He'd specifically told her to stay out of it. But she couldn't resist just doing whatever the hell she wanted.

She looked at him with those tearful eyes and he felt

awful. Both for upsetting her, and for the fact she'd ever found out enough about the business side of things to get to this point. She was quite literally invested now. And she was right, she had actually bought him some more time. With those payments made, he didn't have to look at an immediate sale.

Sam knew he should be grateful. He was grateful. But he was mad too—and scared. Scared that she'd end up resenting him when he lost her money. It was enough stress with Magda to take care of, but now Marnie had dumped all her cash into the place too. She should have bought her own home. Instead, she'd paid off part of his.

"You really should have talked to me, little girl."

"No. Talking doesn't do shit. Paying bills does. I don't know how to horse very well, but I can transfer money. So I did. And I'm not sorry and I won't be sorry either." She folded her arms over her chest and looked up at him with her lower lip stuck out more than she probably realized.

She was adorable. But she was wrong. She'd be very sorry by the time he was done with her. That first little spanking hadn't been enough. It was never enough when it came to Marnie. He knew exactly what she needed and yet he found himself pulling back when it came time to deliver because it was easy to feel sorry for her, and because she always seemed to have a good reason for her disobedience—but enough was enough. Everything about her tone and attitude just begged for correction.

"We'll see about that." he said as he started to roll up his sleeves.

"Sam! No! I can't be in trouble for this!" Marnie started arguing immediately, as usual. This girl could argue the hind leg off a Clydesdale and still not be done.

"I told you to stay out of this, and you went behind my back," he said as he reached out to take her by the arm, wrapping his long fingers around her slim wrist. She was so much smaller than him, so delicate in so many ways—and damn tough in a lot of others.

Prepared to deal with her properly this time, he pulled her squirming, complaining body back over his thighs. Marnie was not going quietly on this one, but Sam was determined. Now, more than ever, she needed to know he was still in charge. Her jeans provided more protection than she really deserved, but he started with them on, his palm finding her ass with satisfying firm slaps that made her yelp.

"Sam! This isn't fair!" she squealed as his hand branded her butt.

"It's very fair. You disobey, you get spanked. I outlined that the first day we met, Marnie."

"I was trying to do something nice!"

"Maybe you were, but your money is for you."

"My money is for doing what I want, and I wanted you help you, dumbass!"

The sentiment was sweet, but the language was so disrespectful he spanked her harder and faster, making damn sure she knew she wasn't going to get out of being disciplined just because she threw money around. Marnie howled, her socked toes drumming against the floor with every single one of the rapid-fire slaps.

Sam grabbed the back of her jeans and yanked them down. Her panties came with them, dragged down her thighs so her sweet curvy ass was exposed. It was a light pink colour, but he intended to make it bright red. She was going to pay for that mouth of hers.

"Sam!" She squealed his name like a plea as the sharper slaps landed across her hindquarters, every single one of them leaving a hot red handprint against her skin that faded into the growing red hue of her bottom as a whole.

There was pleasure in this, in having a reason to give her a damn good spanking and make sure it was one she couldn't forget. Throwing the amount of money she had around was not a smart move. He could easily lose it all, and then where would she be? Jobless, homeless, and without a dollar to her name.

"Sam! Fuck! That hurts!" He could hear the pain in her

voice. It didn't stop him from landing another hard slap to her sweet cheeks. Sadistic? Yeah. Maybe. Earned? Absolutely. Sam was the master of his domain, and Marnie was going to find her place in it or be a very, very sore girl.

He had given her plenty of warnings in the past, tastes of what he was capable of, and she kept coming back for more. She was pushing his limits, so he was happy to push hers right back.

Speaking of… He pushed her far leg off his lap and looped his other leg around it, trapping her with her sex spread over his hard thigh. He could see her sweet pussy gleaming with the arousal she probably wasn't aware of yet. Her ass probably hurt too much to notice that she was soaking, but the wet patch on his jeans didn't lie.

Sam aimed his slaps lower, catching her sensitive inner thighs, moving ever closer to that perfect pouting pink slit of hers.

Her wails and moans reached higher pitches, but she still hadn't said the magic word yet. *Sorry* was exceptionally absent from every single one of her shouts and cries. There wasn't an apology even beginning to form. She was demanding he stop, but he had no intention of giving into her demands, no more than he would have given into any other stroppy filly who stamped her hooves and tried to get her own way.

Marnie learned a lot slower than the horses. Then again, he didn't spank them. Leather and ropes. That's what a truly spirited little mare needed. He didn't have any rope with him, but he did have leather. Grabbing her wrists up behind her, he held them pinned behind her back, giving her a very brief reprieve as he worked one handed at his belt, then slid it from the loops with a *swiiiisshh* that made her bottom quiver.

"Sam!"

His name was delicious on her lips as he doubled the leather over, then brought it down across the centre of her ass in a hard lash, which instantly made a red stripe blaze across her flesh.

"Sam!" She screamed his name, a note of real desperation entering her tone. He paused before he let the next stroke fly.

"I know it hurts, little girl," he said, his voice low and calm. "But you're not learning your lesson. I look after you. You do as I say. It's very simple, Marnie."

"Please! Don't use the belt again!"

Sam let the leather trail lightly over her cheeks. Maybe he was being too mean. Maybe this was too much for her. His cock was hard as hell against the ridge of his fly and he was dying to fuck one of those tight little holes currently on display. The smaller, darker one was calling him.

He dipped a finger down the cleft of her ass and found that bud, touching her in a place he was sure she didn't let men touch her usually.

"Oh, my god." Her muffled little moan didn't exactly sound entirely unenthusiastic.

"Why did you pay that bill, Marnie?"

"Because you needed it paid."

"Right, but you don't care about this place, do you?" He laid the belt across her ass as he questioned her, keeping his middle finger moving in a slow circle around her tight little hole.

"I care," she moaned. The pain was not making her arousal abate one bit. If anything, that lash of the belt had heightened her desire. She could barely keep her hips and ass still as she moved against his thigh in a slow gyration.

"Why?"

"Because..." She trailed off, and he pressed his finger a little harder against the bud of her bottom.

"Why, Marnie?" He let his voice drop into a dominant growl, his index finger dropping down to swipe some of her natural lubrication up against her ass before returning his middle finger to the task of teasing her hole.

"Because I want to stay here!"

"Why?"

"Because I just do, isn't that enough?"

"No." He picked up the belt again and laid another harsh lash across her ass, right next to the first one. She squealed and bucked, but settled down again when his finger went back to her bottom hole. "Tell me why you want to stay here, Marnie. Don't you lie to me, little girl. Don't you hide another thing from me."

She took a few deep sobbing breaths before she managed to reply.

"Because of you..." Her voice was soft, but he heard her clearly. He felt his heart swell and his dick throb. Fuck. He hadn't known how much he'd wanted to hear that until she said it. There was so much longing in her voice, so much sweetness—and so much desire.

"Because you want to be mine?" He wrapped an arm underneath her neck and pulled her up so she was arched, her eyes meeting his as he leaned over to look down at her, his finger making slow headway into her tight little asshole. "Is that what you want, Marnie? Do you want to be my little girl? My little fuck toy?"

"Yesss..." There was a guttural desperation in her hissed reply. He saw her eyes fogged with arousal. He saw her mouth hanging open a little, just begging to be kissed. Her bottom was giving way, letting him enter. Sam pushed his finger slowly inside her tight little ass, using his index finger to push inside the warm velvety embrace of her cunt at the same time.

"You don't understand what being mine is really like, little girl. I can be a very mean daddy."

"I know," she whimpered adorably.

"You know a little," he growled. "But you don't know everything. If you want to be mine, every single one of these holes is going to be mine too. You're going to hold your little ass open and ask your daddy to fuck it, understand?"

He felt her pussy and ass clench at the same time. Oh, she was loving this. Her pussy was absolutely soaked, and her ass was perfectly tight around his finger. He couldn't wait to push his cock inside that hole, and see what that did to the naughty little brat from the city.

• • • • • • •

"Yes, Daddy, I understand." Marnie's voice was a breathless whisper as she forced out the words that made her tummy clench with desire. It felt so naughty to say it, so forbidden to be calling her lover 'Daddy.' And what he planned to do to her… that was even naughtier. And yet it felt so right. Where his finger was, *right there*, pushing inside her bottom hole, did delicious things to her body. Sensations ricocheted through her; sensations she'd never felt before. Her nipples were too tight against her bra and strained to be released. Sam's words went round and round in her head. Had he made her a promise or was it meant to be a threat? She didn't know.

Electricity zinged down her spine, making her tremble, and the sparks exploded where his hand lay in the curve of her ass, his fingers filling both her holes, his words and his actions already claiming her as his.

"What do you want, Marnie? What do you want to be? Tell me. Let me hear you say the words." Sam's voice was a low growl, still, as he stared into her eyes.

Her ass was on fire, the tight skin burning and throbbing, but she couldn't keep her aching pussy from clenching around his finger, nor could she ignore the sensations rippling through from her virgin bud that Sam had plundered. She was still sniffling from the sting of the belt, but she took a deep, shuddering breath.

"I want to be your little girl, Daddy. I want to be your fuck toy." Just saying the words nearly tipped her over the edge. Her swollen clit throbbed against his hand as he delved deep inside her, her juices saturating her thighs and his jeans. The pain in her backside wasn't dimming her arousal even the tiniest bit.

Sam released the hold he had on her neck, allowing

Marnie to collapse down over his thighs. She bit back a sob as the edge of his thumbnail pressed into the scorched skin of her ass. She couldn't breathe, the air was too thick to swallow into her lungs. There was no escape from the sensations roaring through her as he grabbed a handful of her hair in his other hand and tugged.

"Mine," he growled softly. "All mine."

The finger in her pussy started moving, a slow rotation that made her core quiver and twist in anticipation, her arousal deepening with every tiny movement. He slid it deeper inside her, right up to the knuckle. A low moan escaped her throat.

More tears sprang into her eyes as Sam yanked her head back by her hair, his touch not at all gentle now. She couldn't see him properly; tears blurred her vision. But she could taste his mouth on hers, she could feel his stubble scratching her cheek as he pressed his lips on hers, claiming her in a hungry kiss that stole her breath and momentarily took away her pain. The kiss wasn't tender; it was rough and urgent, taken rather than given. But her throbbing pussy clenched around his finger even tighter, another gush of liquid trickled down her already slick thighs. Still holding her hair tightly, his lips still locked to hers, Sam pulled his other hand away from her suddenly, leaving her feeling empty, wanting, body trembling.

She hissed in pain as he rubbed his palm, sticky with her juices, over her burning bottom, tracing the welts he'd made with the belt with his wet finger. The finger that had just seconds ago been inside her. Cupping her hot bottom, he squeezed, then she felt him reach down and dip his finger into her dewy wetness, bringing it back to spread over her tight rosebud that she could feel puckering desperately in response to his touch. She couldn't move, he held her fast. It was torture. Exquisite torture.

"Aaargh! Sam!" Marnie bucked and squealed as Sam pushed his finger inside her ass once again, pushing it in to the hilt this time, making her take it all. Her jerky movement was restricted by Sam's hold on her hair and she froze, her whole body rigid, her bottom clenched, every muscle in her body tense. She tried to expel his finger, to push against it, but he was too strong for her.

"You're mine, little girl," Sam growled. "This hole right here belongs to *me*."

Marnie moaned, a long, low moan that was a mixture of both pleasure and pain, torment and elation. Electricity surged down her spine, exploding when it got to her pelvis, spreading and intensifying, nearly sending her into orbit.

"Yes, Daddy!" she squealed.

She sucked in a breath as Sam drenched a second finger in her juices, dipping it inside her to coat it thoroughly, then ran it around the entrance to her tight hole, the one already plundered by one finger.

"Nooooooo." Her protest sounded more like a moan, which Sam ignored, choosing instead to press his second finger inside her, just the tip at first, then twisting it, spreading her wide to accommodate him. Marnie hissed at the burning signalling the entrance of Sam's digit, but as she pressed back against him, and he pushed his finger in further, the discomfort eased and she slowly relaxed.

Sam released the hold on her hair and she sank her head downward, mortified by her predicament, but excited at the same time. She clutched the leg of his jeans, her nails digging into his calves as she tried frantically to keep herself still. She felt so naughty, enjoying this. Like a wanton slut. She begged him silently to take her properly, to fuck her senseless, to bring her right to the edge of the abyss and let her fly over, rather than leave her like this, dangling, helpless, wet.

What was he doing? He was moving, his upper body heavy against her back. She felt him lean down, almost squashing her, then she gasped, both startled and aroused, as he touched his lips to her punished bottom in the barest of kisses. His lips lightly grazed over the burning welts but even that small touch was too much and she bucked against him.

"No." His flattened hand came down sharply on the back of her thigh, reinforcing his demand. "Let Daddy kiss it better."

The wave of emotions and sensations that flooded her was overwhelming. She couldn't make sense of them as pain, pleasure, humiliation, despair, and longing all jostled for place inside her, tossing her upside down and turning her inside out, so the only thing she was aware of was Sam's fingers, slowly circling, deep in her bottom.

"Oh, god. Sam, please!" Every nerve in her body was on fire as she begged for what she craved, what she so desperately needed. "Please fuck me, Sam. Please!" Marnie could barely contain the pressure that was building inside her as Sam's circling fingers kept up their slow dance, spreading her wider, wider, preparing her bottom for his cock.

"Please." The word came out as a groan. "Please! I can't bear it anymore!"

"What can't you bear, little girl?" Sam's voice was gruff, teasing, fuelling the flames that consumed her.

"This!" she squealed as the finger inside her pussy reached upward, hitting that secret spot that did amazing things to her, at the same time as the fingers in her ass spread her wider, stretching her. "I need you inside me," she begged.

"You'll need to be a bit more specific, little girl. Do you want another finger?"

"No. Your… your cock," she gasped, struggling to speak, struggling to breathe, struggling to think. "I want to feel your cock inside me. Please!"

"Beg."

"Please!" The guttural moan that escaped from her lips was unlike any sound Marnie had ever heard herself make before. Everything was sizzling, every part of her was alive with sensation. If Sam denied her release for too much longer she was certain she would go crazy.

"What do you want me to do, little girl?" Sam's slow, lazy voice drove her even wilder.

"Fuck me. I want you to fuck me."

"Where?" Sam pulled away the hand that was filling her, before touching the tip of his finger to her labia, circling her swollen lips, tapping her wet clit. "Here?"

"No."

"Then where?" The shivers zipping down her spine intensified as Sam's fingertip increased in speed, rubbing her throbbing clit.

"My bottom," she whispered. "Please, Daddy, fuck my bottom hole." Just saying the words felt shameful, but an erotic thrill shot through her at the same time.

Sam lifted her off his lap and shifted, so he was behind her. "Get up on the bed," he commanded hoarsely, "knees wide. Reach back and grab your ass, spread it wide, show me your little hole."

Pressing her forehead into the bed, Marnie braced herself and reached back, just as Sam had instructed. Her bottom felt hot to touch, as she knew it would, and it stung as she pressed her fingers into her scalded skin.

"Hold your ass open, little girl, open wide." Sam's voice was husky with arousal, the passion blurring the words, making them hard to understand.

Ignoring the sting as best she could, Marnie pulled her ass cheeks apart, exposing herself to her daddy, opening herself up wide, just for him, just as he'd asked.

"What do you say, little girl?"

Sam took a step back. He wasn't touching her, but she could feel his eyes on her, claiming her.

Marnie took a deep breath.

"Please fuck me, Daddy," she begged softly. "Please fuck my ass."

Behind her, she heard the rustle of clothing as Sam shed his pants and boxers, leaving them in a puddle on the floor. She felt him grab her hips, felt him press his thighs against her hot bottom. She felt his cock at the entrance to her tight hole. She held her breath.

She trembled, just slightly, as he dipped his cock into her juices, running his thick shaft up and down her slit, coating it thoroughly in the sticky substance.

"Who owns this ass?" he growled in her ear.

"You do, Daddy."

"That's right, little girl. This ass belongs to me."

Sam wasn't gentle as he entered her and she hissed in pain at the burn. He plunged in deeply, his muscular thighs hard up against her bottom. For a moment he was still, letting her get used to his size, then he started to move. Slowly at first, long, deep rhythmic thrusts that tantalized and teased, but quickly grew in pace and intensity.

He picked up her hands, pulling them away from her. "Put them on the bed beside you."

It was easier to balance with her hands next to her, and she used her arms to push herself up a bit more, arching her back, giving Sam better access, offering herself to him fully. He took full advantage of her offering, plunging deeply into her, claiming her completely.

She cried out as he grabbed her hair, pulling her head back again, so far back that the back of her head touched the spot between her shoulder blades.

"So beautiful," he whispered. "So nice and tight."

Marnie glowed at his praise.

Reaching around her hips, Sam found her swollen clit and flicked it softly, quickly, plundering her ass faster and harder.

Marnie was going to explode. She could feel it. Every single nerve in her body was on the brink of combusting. One more flick, one more thrust... "Oh, god, Sam!" she screamed as she flew over the edge, making everything shatter inside her. She couldn't see anything, couldn't breathe, couldn't focus on anything except the sensations devouring her body, churning inside her, erupting.

Wave after wave of the most incredible orgasm she'd ever had washed over her and she thought it would never end. Sam shuddered behind her and his hot seed filled her, spilling out of her, as he collapsed against her, spent.

"Dammit, little girl, you're incredible."

Sore but sated, Marnie rested her head on the bed as a slow smile spread across her face.

CHAPTER NINE

From that moment on, Marnie worked harder than she ever had in her life. Most of the business' problems, as far as she was concerned, were marketing. It was one thing to take people on breath-taking treks, but if nobody knew the place existed, that was a problem.

The current website had been made on an old free web builder sometime in the 1990s and had never been updated. Marnie put her skills to good use, even with intermittent internet that came over the phone lines and downloaded every image painfully slowly.

During the day she worked with the horses and Sam and at night, she slaved over the internet side of things. Sam was encouraging, though he didn't really seem to fully understand what she was doing, and he definitely didn't understand the value of it.

"You don't even have a Facebook page? Instagram? Snapchat?"

He looked at her blankly.

"You must have heard of Facebook," she said. "Nobody gets away with not knowing Facebook."

He gave a little shrug. He wasn't really listening anyway. He was watching the rugby. The All Blacks were playing

Australia and it was a national point of pride that they won. Losing to the Aussies was like a spear right through the heart of the country, and Sam and Magda were glued to the television.

Marnie hadn't ever really been a rugby sort of girl, but it was cute that Sam liked it. He was such a bloke.

"I'm going to start you a Facebook page."

"Yes!" Sam exploded off the couch, shaking his fist in victory. Marnie felt a fraction of a second of pleasure, then she realized it wasn't her work he was so pleased about, it was some guy having carried a ball over a line. The All Blacks had scored a try. Woo fucking hoo.

"Yeah, just ignore me. It's not like I'm trying to save your business or anything," she muttered to herself, rolling her eyes as she turned back to the computer, which had a CRT screen and ran on a version of Windows so old, Clippy was practically her boyfriend now.

"What was that, little girl?"

She glanced over to see Sam's blue eyes catching her in a piercing look. So he had been listening, even if he didn't seem like it. Sam always noticed the things she expected him to miss. She really couldn't get away with anything. In fact, she bet he knew exactly what Facebook was.

"Nothing," she lied.

"You've spent enough time on that computer today," he decided. "Come and relax."

"Not yet," she said absent-mindedly. She was already back into the flow of things. The reception out here was nonexistent, so her phone had been basically useless since she got to Sam's place. It wasn't until he dug out this old computer and got her an internet account that she realized how much she had missed out on. Besides, the business was about ten years behind in its marketing, and they were on a tight schedule. They needed bookings and lots of them if they were going to stave off the dairy conglomerate.

"Now, Marnie."

She ignored him. Back home, she could have uploaded

pictures from her phone straight to her laptop. Here, it was tedious process of transferring images from a camera to the PC via a USB cable that ran almost as slowly as the internet did.

Marnie squealed as powerful arms wrapped around her unexpectedly.

"That's enough," Sam said, physically picking her up and off the computer. "You're done for the night, little girl."

"No, Sam! I'm not. I need to upload and tag and share, and then I need to cross-post to a few sites and..."

"You can download your uploads tomorrow," Sam said, tossing her over his shoulder as if she didn't weigh anything more than your average bale of hay. "It's bedtime."

"Magda!" Marnie called out to Sam's aunt, but the woman merely looked up from her knitting and smiled. Magda was firmly team Sam. Dammit.

"But the All Blacks haven't won yet! Don't you want to know what the score is?"

"You need to know the score more than I do," Sam growled, carrying her up the stairs. "Disobeying me, giving me attitude, ignoring me... none of that is acceptable, Marnie."

"I was *working!*"

"I'm the boss and I say you've done enough work for one day," Sam said evenly. He deposited Marnie at the top of the stairs and smacked her bottom to encourage her toward the bathroom. The sharp sting didn't improve Marnie's mood any, but she didn't want to test Sam, so she did as she was told and scurried in to brush her teeth.

When she emerged, he was waiting for her.

"What? What did I do now?"

"You're sleeping with me," he said flatly. "It's about time we shared a bed. And I don't want you sneaking back downstairs to do that internet stuff. We have real work to do in the morning."

"That *is* real work, Sam!"

He didn't get it, and that more than annoyed her.

"You can have all the farms in the universe, you can have horses coming out of your ass, but if you don't tell people about it, nobody knows! The internet is important, Sam. It could be the key to saving this place."

"It won't be the key to saving it tonight," he said firmly. "And you're going to be mucking out all the stalls tomorrow as punishment for that attitude. Do you want to do it with a sore ass?"

No. She didn't. And sleeping in the same bed as Sam did sound nice. They hadn't really done that yet. It was sort of the final step of 'moving in.' Kiwi couples were notorious for falling into relationships largely by accident. Marnie had once been with a guy for six months after they were mistakenly booked into the same hotel room.

Her relationship with Sam hadn't been quantified yet. Were they boyfriend and girlfriend? She didn't know. Sam didn't exactly treat her or date her. He spanked her and fucked her instead. And now he had her by the arm and was marching her to bed, apparently tired of the argument.

"Get in bed and go to sleep," he ordered, pulling back the cover. She didn't really have a choice, so she got in and sat there as he got ready for bed, stripping off his rugby jersey and his jeans to reveal the hard lines of his body. He was wearing boxers that stayed on, but other than that he was utterly naked. God, he was hot. She'd never get over his muscles. Washboard abs rippling with the most pedestrian of motions. He could make brushing his teeth look like a peep show.

Hot enough that she almost forgot she was mad at him. He slid into bed next to her and flicked out the light, leaving her annoyed and a little aroused.

"Sam…"

"Go to sleep, Marnie," he rumbled.

"I can't sleep."

He rolled over onto his back and she saw his eyes pale in the little bits of moonlight sneaking through the curtains. "What is it?"

"What are we going to do if we can't save this place? Are we… are you and I…" She couldn't quite form the question, but it was simple. Was he going to get rid of her? Would they go their separate ways? Was this a real thing, or just a relationship of kink and convenience to him?

"I'm not letting you go, little girl," he rumbled, leaning over to press a chaste, affectionate kiss to her cheek. "Now get some sleep. You have to be up in a few hours."

Marnie nodded and closed her eyes.

"Sam?"

"What?"

"We are going to save this place, right?"

She heard him sigh. "Go to sleep, Marnie."

Marnie closed her eyes tighter. Nothing was guaranteed, and they both knew it. Sam called her little girl, but he wasn't treating her like one now. He didn't lie, or pretend everything was going to be okay. They'd try their best, and that was it. He was right. She really did need her sleep.

· · · · · · ·

"Stalls, Marnie." Sam handed her a rake and pointed her toward the wheelbarrow. It was six-thirty in the morning and they had a few people coming in for a trek today. They'd gotten one of the fliers Marnie had gone to Culverden to print out and leave at the dairy counter.

She didn't cry over having to muck out anymore. Dirt and horseshit was becoming part of her experience. That didn't mean she liked it. It was real physical labour, the kind of exercise that made a gym entirely unnecessary.

"So unfair," she complained.

Sam's hand connected with her jean-clad ass with a solid whack. "Get to work. Now."

Marnie stuck her tongue out at him, but went to do as she was told. Sam was a steady influence in these hard times. He rarely let the strain of the situation show, especially not when the horses or clients were around. He was as charming and cheerful with them as ever.

Some of the women liked to flirt with Sam. Most of the women did, in fact, though most of the time it was innocent enough. More than one lady perfectly capable of clambering into a saddle would hem and haw on the mounting block and bat their lashes until Sam came and put their foot into the stirrup.

That morning there was one particularly pathetic specimen of a woman who looked limber as a gymnast but insisted that she had no idea how to get onto the saddle.

"You know how to sit down, right?" Marnie tried to keep the growl out of her voice.

"I think it's better if the professional assists me," the lady said, her voice haughty with the particular attempt at an upper class accent some rich people liked to put on. It never worked. There was no point trying to sound like fancy kiwi.

The lady looked down her nose at Marnie, a particular derision in her gaze that spoke volumes without her having to say a word. This woman thought Marnie was beneath her. Marnie scowled. When Marnie had first come to the farm, she'd looked better than this Merivale cougar with her perfect makeup, straightened hair, and super-tight leggings that showed every curve and inner fold she had. Sam hadn't approved of her clothing, but at least she hadn't showed up with a camel toe. Now she was dressed in dusty jeans and a dirty shirt, her hair was all mussed up, and she hadn't put on makeup in days.

"It's so hard to get good help these days," the woman remarked to her friend.

"Excuse me, bitch?"

The woman gasped in shock, as if she'd never heard a swear word before. The moment the word was out of Marnie's mouth, she knew she'd made a mistake. She was tired and grumpy and not in the mood for people being rude to her, but that wasn't any excuse. At least Sam hadn't heard…

"Marnie. Barn. Now."

Marnie turned around to see Sam standing behind her, his arms folded, a knee-quiveringly serious expression on his face.

She put her head down and went to the barn, knowing she was in deep shit. Sam followed after her, and once they were out of sight of the customers, slapped her ass hard enough to make her yelp, then grabbed her arm and practically dragged her into the office.

"What the hell do you think you're doing?"

"She was trying to hit on you," Marnie growled. "And she was rude to me!"

"So you insulted a client? While we're trying to save this place you think it's a good idea to call customers names?"

"If they fit," Marnie shrugged.

"I will deal with you later, little girl," Sam said sternly. "I'm not holding the ride over this—but you are in trouble."

Marnie bit her lower lip as Sam strode away.

It wasn't fair! That up-herself woman out there *was* a bitch. She was old enough to be Sam's mother yet she was unabashedly hitting on him! Marnie growled under her breath as she sank down into Sam's swively chair. It *so* wasn't fair! Marnie had worked hard all morning. She'd mucked out stables, saddled up horses, worked her guts out, to help Sam. Now that Merivale cougar out there got to go riding with Sam while Marnie did… well… nothing. She glanced around Sam's office. He'd obviously had a clean-out since she'd accidentally found that letter from the bank. Now there were no papers anywhere that she could see; there was nothing at all. The office was virtually empty. There was literally nothing for her to do.

Marnie yawned. Since discovering just how close to losing this place Sam was, she hadn't slept properly, and it was starting to catch up with her. Leaning right back in Sam's chair, she put her booted feet up on Sam's desk and closed her eyes. While there was nothing for her to do, she may as well make the most of it and relax.

A loud bang, then voices, woke her up. Rubbing her

eyes, Marnie took her feet off Sam's desk and straightened up. Should she go and help Sam unsaddle the horses? *No,* she decided. *He can do it himself.* She really didn't want to see that nasty woman again, and if she was in trouble anyway, there was no point in putting herself into Sam's presence any earlier than she had to.

The commotion eased outside; the trekkers had obviously gone. Sam was fumbling around somewhere in the barn, but he didn't come in. Surely he wasn't still mad at her?

Marnie got out of the chair. This was ridiculous. She hadn't been that bad! Butterflies fluttered furiously in her tummy as she peeped around the corner, apprehensive about facing Sam's wrath. *I'll deal with you later, little girl* echoed round and round in her head.

Sam was at the other end of the barn, near the door, when she poked her head around the corner just in time to see him shed his shirt and throw it carelessly on top of a bale of hay against the wall. A catch-all, it was piled with riding crops and helmets, and now his shirt. He strode outside wearing nothing but his jeans. Even from this distance, she could see the muscles rippling in his back. Where was he going dressed like that? He was always telling her to cover up, to protect herself from the hot Canterbury sun. Good advice, but why did it suddenly not apply to him?

Marnie watched as he grabbed a couple of items off a barrel standing just outside the main barn door. What were they? She couldn't see. Scurrying down the wide aisle of the barn as quietly as she could, she crept closer, her curiosity piqued.

Rope. Dangling from his left hand was a coil of rope. From the other, a stock whip. A shiver went down Marnie's spine. What did he have in mind? Both of those items had multiple potential uses, many of which would not bode well for her. She held her breath, debating whether or not to run. If she had any sense, she would run. But she couldn't make her feet move; they were stuck fast to the ground. She fully expected Sam to turn around and see her, to tie her up and whip her senseless… but he didn't. Instead, he walked over to his horse, still holding both the rope and the whip, and mounted.

Marnie's heart was in her mouth as Sam sat in the saddle, tall and straight, proud, like he belonged there. The sun glinted off his muscular torso. Damn, the man was ripped! She could grate cheese on those abs! His skin was evenly tanned. Despite the sun protection advice he drummed into her, he clearly ignored it on occasion.

The muscles in Sam's arm and shoulder flexed impressively as he raised the whip high above his head, flicking his wrist forward and backward quickly, cracking the whip. It sounded like a gunshot and Marnie jumped, grabbing hold of the barn door to steady herself.

Fred didn't move.

Sam flicked his wrist again, cracking the whip directly above his head, then he bent his arm, changing the angle of the whip, cracking it behind him, then in front, slicing the long grass next to Fred's feet. Marnie couldn't take her eyes off him. The way his muscles jumped with every tiny movement had her mesmerized.

Shifting position against the wall, her arm pressed against something hard against her boob. Her phone! She'd forgotten about that! She was so used to carrying it with her for so long that even though it didn't work out here hardly at all, it was a matter of habit to just pick it up, tuck it inside her bra, and take it with her wherever she went that she did it without thinking. She did use it to take pictures occasionally, and uploaded them to Facebook when she went into Culverden to use the internet, but that was about it. But now, it was perfect. Scrolling through the home screen quickly, she touched the camera app. This was something she might never get to see again, especially not if Sam gave up fighting.

Bringing the phone lens into focus, Marnie braced herself solidly against the barn, trying to still her shaking hands enough to clearly video Sam. The muscles in his arm and shoulder bulged as he cracked the whip again, building up a rhythm, *crack, crack, crack... crack, crack, crack...* like the beat of a song. The whip moved so quickly she could hardly follow it, and the whip cracks pierced the air, sending chills through her.

Slowly, Sam started to spin the rope he held, twirling the lasso into a big loop above his head. He spun the rope faster and faster, his upper body moving gracefully in a perfect rhythm. At the same time, he kept up with the whip, cracking it high, low, behind him, in front, slowly, quickly, repeating the same beat over and over again.

Marnie couldn't breathe, she couldn't move. Her breasts felt heavy, achy, her nipples hard. Her lady parts throbbed with arousal. She couldn't take her eyes off Sam. The way each arm moved in a different direction, yet in the same rhythm, his pelvis shifting in time with the movements, his muscles flexing, was incredible.

The rhythm was perfect; Sam didn't miss a beat. Still twirling the rope above his head, he picked up the pace of the whip a bit, double-cracking it on the downward stroke as he flung the long strip of leather out behind him, then brought it back past his body with another crack. How did the rope and the whip not get tangled up? Both of them were in the air at once, moving at high speed, but with so much precision. Once again, Sam was totally in control.

Fred started moving, just a walk at first. Sam's back was to her now, but he was no less impressive. The muscles rippling in his back turned her on just as much as his abs did, and his shoulders were even better defined from this angle. Marnie was frozen, unable to look away.

They turned then, heading back toward her, and Sam saw her watching. His eyes locked on hers. She had the rhythm of the whip in her head now, and as she returned Sam's gaze, that rhythm never wavered. Nor did the spinning of the rope. Sam looked more powerful than she'd ever seen him before.

"Marnie," he called over the cracking of the whip, his voice clear and even. "Come here."

She sucked in a breath, and took one tiny step forward. Then another. Then another. Fred continued to walk toward her. Sam cracked the whip slower now, in time with Fred's steps, his eyes still fixed on hers. She wanted to back away, to turn and run... but she couldn't. The spinning, the cracking, the impressive display of masculine perfection had her hypnotized.

Marnie's chest was tight and the butterflies inside her were going crazy. Her palms were clammy, the phone was slippery. The gusset of her knickers grew damper with each step she took.

Suddenly, the rhythm of the whip changed. Instead of keeping time with Fred, Sam raised his arm higher and cracked the whip quickly, *crack, crack, crack, crack, crack* in quick succession. Before she knew what was happening, he threw the rope, the loop landing perfectly around her waist, tying her arms to her sides. Fred backed up, tightening the noose. The whip continued to crack, landing closer and closer to her with each loud report. She could see the grass being sliced just in front of her. She pulled back, but found she was held fast.

She tried to shriek, but no sound came out; she was helpless, powerless. Paralyzed. Not just by fear, but by arousal. The whip, the rope, the muscles, the whole package was the hottest thing she'd seen, ever.

Sam cracked the whip again, landing the lash right between her feet. He tugged on the rope looped tightly around her middle.

"Come to Daddy, little girl," he growled. "You are in so much trouble!"

Held tightly in the leather bonds, Marnie was dragged to within just a few inches of Sam's hard body. He glared down at her, his muscles gleaming in the setting sun, playing off the light sheen of sweat and dust. He smelled like horses and man musk.

"I don't need to tell you that calling a customer a bitch is a bad idea, do I?" He growled the question, his blue eyes so stern she wished she could fall through the earth. Not that it would have worked. He would have caught her with this whip and dragged her right back, even from the gates of hell. There was no way of getting away from Sam once he set his sights on you. That made her afraid and secure all at the same time.

"Well…"

"The answer is no, little girl," he growled, the muscle in his jaw clenching. "The answer is always no."

"Yes, Daddy."

She saw his eyes flash with arousal. He liked it when she called him Daddy, but she didn't do it often because it made her feel small and embarrassed. Not right now though. Right now it felt right, and a little bit necessary.

"What am I going to do with you?" He purred the question, his blue eyes flashing. They both knew he already had the answer.

· · · · · · ·

Goddamn. She deserved a whipping for what she'd said to that woman. He'd known Marnie had a mouth on her, but she'd still managed to shock him with that display of temper. Hearing her call a paying customer a bitch would be a moment he'd never forget. He knew she had city standards when it came to her behaviour, and he wasn't above swearing himself, but not to a woman who was paying their way. That was utterly unacceptable. If she was just an employee, she'd be getting a written warning. As his little girl, she was going to get a whole lot more than that.

Her sudden complete submission threw him off a bit. The word 'daddy' coming out of her mouth made his cock rock hard. Unfortunately for Marnie, Sam enjoyed punishing her almost as much as he liked fucking her, and Marnie calling him Daddy wasn't going to get her out of this. It was just going to make it more satisfying for the both of them.

"I only said that to her because she was trying to get with you."

The pouty, sulky excuses had begun. He'd wondered where they were.

"You think I'm going to leave you for some random woman who can't get on a horse?"

"Well, no..."

"So you just wanted to claim your territory?"

"I don't know." Marnie looked at her toes. "She was really rude to me, she looked at me like I was nothing, like just some messy, ugly farm girl."

"Hey." Sam reached out and tipped her chin back up. "That's because she was a snob. How she treats you reflects on her, not you, and you know better than to act out like that. At least, I hope you do."

"Yeah, I know," Marnie admitted, her eyes sliding to the side. She was doing her best to avoid his gaze. Every time she looked at him, her cheeks blushed in that adorable way, and her eyes shone a little brighter. This punishment had more than one purpose. He didn't just need to teach her not to swear at customers. He also needed to teach her that she wasn't bloody well replaceable with the first overly made-up woman who batted her fake eyelashes at him.

It was just as well Marnie hadn't been on the ride, because that woman had spent the entire time trying to get his attention. It hadn't worked. He wasn't interested in anyone besides Marnie. She was the only woman he thought of, the only one he wanted. And the fact that she didn't seem to know that worried him more than the swearing.

"You, young lady, are everything to me," he said, leaning down and drawing her close, so they were nose to nose and there was nowhere for her to hide. "I love you, Marnie. I could take a trek of naked ladies out and I'd be thinking about you, understand? I'm a one-woman man. And you're my woman. So you don't need to mark your territory, or tell other women off. I'm the one who decides who gets me. And it's you."

She took a deep, quivering breath, and he saw tears forming in her eyes. Happy tears, he thought, given the way her lips were curling up into a little smile.

"Thank you," she said softly. "I really needed to hear that."

"You're not out of trouble," he said. "Not at all. And by the time I'm done with you, little girl, you won't need to hear this because you'll know it. And every time you sit down, you'll be reminded of it."

"Sam…" Her voice was high and pleading. He shook his head. He wasn't going to let her off this one. She really needed to understand what he was saying, and take it to heart. And she needed to know that their relationship wasn't going to be one of those ones with a jealous girlfriend causing chaos and a guy too whipped to do anything about it. He held the whip in this relationship, and he knew how to use it too.

He released the whip with a flick of his wrist, urging the leather to unwrap from her disobedient body. There was a brief moment where triumph—and disappointment—flashed in her eyes, but she was celebrating too soon. He needed the whip off her waist so he could use it on her ass.

"Get into the barn," he ordered. "And bend over a bale. Your choice."

"Sam…"

"Go. Now." He put an authoritative growl in his voice. He wasn't going to be nice about this, even though it was meant to show her she was loved.

She lowered her head, turned around, and did as she was told. He followed after her, staying close behind as she scuffed her way over to a stack of bales, stopped in front of it, turned around and gave him a doe-like look under her lashes.

Sam stayed stern. "Over the bale, Marnie," he said. "And you can pull your pants down too. You're not going to be needing them."

He stood with his arms folded, the whip firmly clenched and coiled in one hand as he waited for her to obey. She made for a sorry sight as her hands went to her pants and started pushing them down.

"Knickers too," he snapped when he saw that she was trying to get around baring her bottom for him. That wasn't going to fly. Naughty girls were punished on the bare, and they were punished long and hard.

She made quite a production out of it, her lower lip sticking out as her ass came into view slowly, her jeans inching down over her ass until she stopped with them just below her beautiful butt. Sam could have watched the show forever, but there was a punishment to give. He stepped forward, hooked his fingers in the back of her jeans and knickers, and yanked them down to her knees, giving her enough of a nudge at the same time that she went face down over the bale of hay and ended up with her ass presented perfectly, two cheeks nice and high, pale for now—but they'd be red soon enough.

"Keep your hands on the ground," he ordered. "Don't move them. You move, we start again."

"Sam…" she whimpered his name again, but Sam wasn't what he wanted to hear. Right now, he was her daddy. Her very displeased daddy who planned to give his little girl the whipping she deserved.

"Quiet, little girl," he growled, uncoiling the whip with a flourish that made the tip snap in the air. "The time for you to talk is over. It's time for you to listen. And feel."

"I'm sorry," she whispered, breaking his rule right away. Sam shook his head and cracked the whip over her head, the tail breaking the sound barrier with a sharp sonic boom that made her jolt in place.

"I said quiet," he repeated. "I'm not playing with you right now, Marnie. This is the most serious punishment I've ever given you, and if you pay attention and learn your lesson, it might be the most serious one you ever get."

He could tell she was just bursting to talk, to apologize, to plead for her ass, but she managed to keep her tongue in check for once. Good. She was learning.

Sam took a few steps back. He needed space to let the whip run out. This was going to be some precision work on a very delicate target. He'd needed to get his eye in if he was going to whip his little girl into shape. That was why he'd started out with a bit of practice before getting Marnie—not that she'd waited to be gotten, of course. She was impatient for everything, including her punishments.

Marnie was terrified, that was obvious by the way she was trembling slightly. But the dewy wetness glistening from that little spot between her thighs told him that she was aroused, too. Her body always responded in a beautiful way to his punishments. It started responding the second he put the steel into his voice. Right now, her palms were flat on the ground in front of her just as he'd instructed, but he knew that wouldn't last long. After just a few lashes of his whip he knew she'd be leaping up, twisting and squirming, trying to avoid what she had coming. He smirked. Maybe he'd have to make use of the rope he'd used to reel her in, to tie her in place.

Taking a deep breath, he shook the whip lightly, adjusting his grip. He couldn't afford to stuff this up. If he missed, Marnie could be hurt, and he didn't want that. Leaning back, he took careful aim, lining the whip up carefully before flicking his wrist, sending the tip flying to land right in the centre of her left buttock. As expected, she screeched when the lash bit into her tender skin and rocked forward, clenching her bottom. Without a pause he let the whip fly again, this time making it bite the same spot on her right buttock. She screamed the second time too, her whole body tensed up and she lifted up off the bale, nearly straightening up.

Sam strode forward, reached down and pressed her back into position. "No, don't move. This has barely started, little girl. Hands back on the ground." She didn't want to obey him; he had to press her firmly to make her bend over the bale again. Her perfect, pale ass was now marred by two distinct red lines, running parallel, one on each cheek. He tossed the whip lightly in his hand. This strip of plaited leather had been in his life for a long time. It came in handy for mustering stock, he could crack the beat of the national anthem, cut the twine on a bale of hay, slice individual blades of grass, and he'd even entered a few whip-cracking contests at A&P shows. But never before had accuracy mattered quite as much as it did now.

Taking his position further back, Sam sent the whip flying again. It cracked it just above her head, the sound echoing loudly through the barn and making her jump.

"I love you, Marnie," he told her, letting the whip fly again, making the tip land just beneath the first one, in a stinging kiss that made her squeal in pain and bolt upright, her hands flying to her backside.

"No, keep still," he growled, coming forward yet again. "Move again, and I'll tie you in place. And we'll start this again, from the beginning. You don't want to make me do that."

A single tear tracked a solitary path down her dusty cheek and he longed to kiss it away. Instead, he brushed it roughly with his thumb, smiling at her gently. "Back into position," he reminded her, the steel gone from his voice.

She obeyed him, her vulnerable position displaying her arousal to him. Her trembling thighs indicated she was afraid, but her glistening sex proved the pleasure was winning out over the pain.

Again he returned to his position. Raising the whip above his head, Sam cracked it twice, quickly, before flicking it out to bite her beautiful ass again. Marnie yelped, but aside from wiggling her hips, she stayed still.

"Good girl," he purred, pleased that she remained in position.

"I'm sorry, Daddy!" she yelled, her voice breaking. Her gentle sobbing almost made him halt the punishment, but a quick glance between her legs at her swollen pussy lips, her hungry clit, made him change his mind. Her ass might be on fire, but her traitorous body was enjoying this whipping. Coiling his whip for a moment, he came back to her, reached down and cupped her dripping mound in his palm, flicking her clit with the tip of his finger. She moaned in response, arching her back, offering herself to him. His rock-hard cock strained against his pants at her lewd display of wanton lust. A growl escaped his throat. He pulled his hand away; she moaned in protest.

He still wasn't done though, not by half. He stepped back into position, leaving her squirming over the hay. Sam flicked out his whip, before raising it high, cracking it above his head, making her jump. It was like a dance where neither of them knew the steps and they had to make it up as they went along, but their bodies flowed together in perfect union, fitting into each other, no matter which direction they moved.

"Such a naughty girl, Marnie."

The air was electric between them. He cracked the whip again, lower this time, directly over her back. He felt the rush of air against his face from the flying lash. Could Marnie feel it too? As he watched, a shiver rippled down her spine. She felt it.

Deftly, he whipped her again, flicking his wrist in a backhanded motion that made the whip crack twice before it connected with her flesh, leaving a bright red stripe directly below the first two.

Marnie gasped and drew her bottom in.

"Do you understand why you're getting punished?" he demanded, his voice harsh, hoarse with arousal.

"Yes, Daddy," she whimpered. "Please, no more! It stings!"

"It's meant to," he responded, his voice a bit softer, but still hoarse. "It's meant to hurt, how else are you going to learn this lesson?"

Twisting his body slightly, he sent the whip flying to snap

against the other side of her ass, adding a third perfect red line. Her ass was gorgeous in its natural creamy white state, but he much preferred it like this, bearing his marks. She bent down, sinking low over the bale, reflexively drawing away from the pain, but after a moment she straightened up without needing to be prompted.

"Good girl." Responding to his praise, she positioned herself perfectly over the bale, her most intimate places on display, vulnerable. He smiled proudly. Her submission to him was the biggest turn-on ever.

"I love you, Marnie," he told her, cracking the whip against her ass again. "Do you hear me?"

"Yes, Daddy," she whimpered, sobbing softly.

Coiling the whip, Sam came forward and ran his palm over her punished bottom, his fingers lingering on the angry, raised red welts. He trailed his thumb down her cleft, stopping at her naughtiest hole, pressing the pad of his thumb against her tight rosebud. She clenched around him, barring his entrance.

"No. Relax," he murmured. Obediently, she did, releasing his thumb. "Good girl."

He held his hand there for a moment longer, pressing lightly against her, using his fingers to rub slow circles over her scorched bottom. Gradually, she relaxed properly beneath his touch, her trembling eased and her sobs quietened. More than anything, he wanted to fuck her, she looked so tempting, bent over like that. But he wasn't done with her yet.

Moving in closer to her, he transferred the whip to his left hand and held it in the small of her back, both holding her in position, and letting the leather fall over her body, reminding her of what was still to come. Bringing his hand back, he slapped her hard, right at the juncture where her bottom met her thighs, and watched in satisfaction as his pink splotchy handprint appeared on her skin.

"You. Do. Not. Swear. At. Paying. Customers," he growled, accompanying each word with a fiery smack.

"I know! I'm sorry!" she yelled.

"You've got a stake in this business now, too, little girl," he reminded her. "We're going to have to work hard, together, if we're going to have any chance of saving it." He smacked her again, with close to his full strength, to drive his message home.

Standing up, he stepped back, letting the end of the whip trail over her lower back, brushing over her backside and kissing her thighs.

"A few more with the whip now, little girl," he told her softly, but firmly. "And after each one, I want to hear you say *Daddy loves me*. Can you do that for me, baby girl?"

"Yes, Daddy." Her words caught on a sob, nearly breaking his resolve, but he steeled himself.

Crack! The whip landed just above the handprints he'd made. "Say it," he growled.

"Daddy loves me!" Marnie shouted.

Crack! "Again!"

"Ow! Daddy loves me!" The words were shrill, yelled, all jumbled together in one breathless outburst, right before she starting crying properly, her whole body racked with sobs.

Crack! "Again!"

He couldn't even understand her this time, the words she yelled were totally unintelligible. She flinched when he stepped forward and touched her bottom, inspecting her skin. She was shaking. Dropping the whip down onto the hay bale next to her, he wrapped an arm around her waist and hauled her to her feet. He spun her to face him and gazed down into her tear-filled eyes. Kissing her forehead tenderly, he brushed loose strands of hair off her wet face before pulling her into his chest.

"Ssssh, baby girl," he soothed. "It's over."

• • • • • • •

She was sore. The whip had left traces of pure fire on

157

her skin and she really wasn't sure she'd ever sit again. But she was loved. She knew it to her core. Marnie had never imagined in a million years that a man could stand over her with a whip in his hand, take the business end of it to her ass, and leave her feeling cherished as well as chastised, but that was exactly what Sam had done.

He slid one hand down her back and scooped her up into his arms, carrying her against his chest. She snuggled her face into his neck, feeling embarrassed and small as he carried her still bare-bottomed self across the open space between the barn and the house, apparently not caring who saw his naughty girl in her well-punished state.

She felt the powerful motion of his body as he carried her up the stairs and into the bedroom they shared. The dated décor and wallpaper curling in places had never seemed as precious as it did as he laid her down carefully on the bed. Marnie wouldn't let go of him when he tried to stand up. Her fingers curled in his hair as she clung to him, afraid that he might make her stay alone. Of all the things in the world, right now, being alone would be the worst.

"Don't leave me."

"It's okay, I'm not going anywhere," he murmured reassuringly. "I was just going to take my pants off."

"Oh. Okay. You can do that." Marnie let go and watched as Sam stood up, unzipped his pants, and got entirely naked. His cock was thick and hard, rampant with the same need she felt and when he came back to lie down next to her, she spread her thighs out of instinct, wrapping herself around him before he even had a chance to fully reach the bed.

"You need something, baby girl?" He murmured the question against her lips, the head of his cock grazing her sex.

She needed him. She needed him more than air. She was so wet she could feel her juices on her inner thighs. The pain of the whip, the humiliation of staying in place and letting herself be punished, had created a state of pure submission and arousal that made her unable to hide her need.

"Please, Daddy," she whimpered, gyrating her hips. The pain of his whip was nothing compared to the arousal coursing through her body. She could feel every place his lash had landed, but the sting and pain only made her want him more.

She heard his growl of desire and a second later the world spun as Sam rolled her onto her back, looked deep into her eyes, and pushed himself inside her, filling her wet pussy in one gloriously long, slow stroke that felt as though it would go on forever. Pinned to the bed, his hand sliding between her breasts to find her neck, Marnie was held down and fucked, Sam's powerful body dominating hers easily with every stroke.

Marnie cried out, her inner walls clenching that thick rod, feeling his fingers clasping firmly around her neck.

"Look at me, little girl," he demanded, his voice thick with a primitive lust that demanded her full obedience.

Looking into his eyes, she saw his love, his desire, and his total and utter control. Sam pushed her legs wide open with his free hand, then placed the base of his palm just above her clit, putting enough pressure on her mound to stretch her pussy for him. It was a lewd, crude display of her sex, and he was using her pussy with little regard for what she wanted in that moment. She had to want what he wanted, and she did. She wanted his thick cock deep inside her. She wanted to be spread open and held wide, she wanted...

"Oh, my..."

He'd pulled out of her pussy, scooping the juices that had been running down the crack of her ass with his cock, he pushed himself against that tight hole.

"Open up for me, baby girl," he murmured, his brilliant blue gaze locked on hers, his fingers tightening around her throat just enough to amplify the order. "Give me your asshole."

With a little whimper, she did the best she could to let her muscles relax. Sam surged forward, pushing the head of his cock past the tight ring of her hole and finding the hot depths of her ass.

"These holes are mine," he reminded her. "All of them. And when you're naughty, you're going to have your bottom fucked, little girl, nice and long and hard."

Marnie moaned as Sam pushed a little further forward. Her ass was so much tighter than her pussy, and her daddy's cock couldn't sink as far or as fast, but he made up for it by reaching down with the hand not wrapped around her neck, and rubbing her pussy.

"Oh, god, oh, yes, please... fuck, yes... Daddy... ow!"

Her eyes flew open wide as Sam's hand left her pussy and the flat of his fingers returned with a swift slap to her lower lips. He was fucking her ass and spanking her pussy at the same time, and there was nothing she could do but lie there, her bottom stretched around his hard cock, her naughty pussy dripping with juices as he spanked her lower lips and all around her clit, swift little taps that made her sensitive lower lips swell up and redden.

"You were a bad girl," he told her gruffly, his abs rippling with every thrust, his perfect shoulders flexing as he fucked her. "But your daddy is always going to be here to deal with you when you're bad."

She was going to come. He wasn't even in her pussy. He was punishing her pussy and fucking her bottom hole and she was still going to come soon. The tight, hot feeling was starting to spread from that secret little place deep inside her. Her clit was tingling, her lips were swelling and stinging, and her ass was surrendering to his cock so now he could fuck her properly, his dick pounding deep inside her over and over.

Fucked and spanked, punished like she was the naughtiest girl in the world, Marnie couldn't hold back anymore. Her whole body was tense and tight, her breath coming in short little gasps, her toes curling and her thighs shaking as she gave in to orgasm.

Marnie looked up into Sam's eyes. He was punishing her.

He was giving her pain with the pleasure. But there was no anger in his gaze. There was the most pure lustful devotion she had ever seen on a man's face. That was what sent her over the edge.

"Daddddyyy!" she cried out as she came, her ass clenching desperately at his cock, the tight ring demanding his cum as pure pleasure burst through her, taking total control of her body—and Sam's too. In that brief moment of climax, it was her female form that ruled them both. His cock was taken in service of her desires and he couldn't resist any more than she could.

Sam roared with orgasm, his palm whipping against her quivering cunt. He drove forward hard and unleashed his cum inside her ass, filling her all the way up with his hot seed. For a minute, there was nothing but orgasm, two writhing bodies caught in a sensation greater than either of them could contain.

Then, slowly, it abated, leaving the hardness of his body, the warmth of his cum, the lashes on Marnie's rear, and the aching of her poor punished pussy.

"Ow," she whimpered softly as he pulled out of her ass, his cock leaving a trail of semen dripping from her well-fucked hole.

"You were such a good girl," he praised, kissing her deeply. She felt his muscular arms wrap around her, comforting her punished body as she curled up against him, still trembling from the force of the orgasm. When Sam fucked you, you knew you'd been fucked. Marnie was certain she wasn't going to walk right for a while.

"I think you need a bath," he said, looking down at her sweaty, cum-stained body. "And I think I need one too."

Once more, he picked her up, carrying her as if she weighed nothing. Marnie was too perfectly exhausted to do more than mumble as Sam took her to the little bathroom and sat her on his knee at the side of the tub as he ran the bath for them both.

"Have you learned your lesson?"

"Yes, Daddy," she murmured, her voice soft. "I won't call any more of the customers bitches."

"Mhm, and more than that, little girl. Do you understand that I love you more than life? That there's nobody else for me but you? And no matter what happens to this place, I'll always be grateful, because I got to meet you?"

Marnie's eyes filled with tears of emotion. She didn't know why he loved her so much, but she was so grateful he did, because she felt exactly the same way. Before coming to the farm, life had been hollow, full of shattered buildings, chaos, and destruction inside and out. Now she was loved, so completely cherished that the entire world could fall down and as long as she had Sam she would be okay.

CHAPTER TEN

One month later…

Marnie knew something was up the moment she came downstairs and saw Sam's face. It wasn't even just his expression, it was his whole posture. Something was dreadfully wrong.

"Sam?" Her voice quivered as she fearfully asked the question. She didn't know what it was she was afraid of, exactly, but something was bothering Sam, and it wasn't anything good.

Before she could get close enough to see what it was he was looking at, he gathered the papers up into a pile and turned them over, hiding them from her view. So it was a secret, then. That was bad.

"Come on." Sam stood up. "Let's get to work." His voice was flat, completely devoid of emotion. He didn't sound happy to be going out to work with the horses, to take out a trek, like he normally did. Right now, he sounded sad. Dejected.

"Something's wrong, isn't it?" she demanded.

Sam sighed.

"Tell me! I'm not going to come and do any work until

you tell me what's going on!" She stamped her foot and pouted, crossing her arms over her chest to prove to Sam that she was serious.

With another sigh, Sam bent down and grabbed her around the waist, slinging her over his broad shoulder like a sack of spuds. "Yes, you are, little girl. We've got a trek coming soon, maybe our last one. And I need your help."

"Put me down, you brute!" she yelled. "What do you mean, our last one? Sam! What's going on?" He didn't release her, so she balled her small hands into fists and pounded against his back. "Sam!" she shouted at him, whacking him as hard as she could. "Talk to me!"

She felt him pause slightly and stiffen. Was he actually going to do as she asked him, for once? No such luck. His big hand crashed down on her backside, making her squeal in outrage and pain. "Stop hitting me, little girl," he snarled. "Yes, this could very well be our last trek." His grip on her thighs shifted slightly, as he bent to put on his boots. Marnie held her breath, both waiting for him to explain himself and fearful of being tipped off. Instead of punching him, she clutched at his shirt, crossing her fingers for good news.

"That paperwork I was reading, it was a letter from the lawyer, and an agreement for me to sign. This place is being sold, Marnie. That big dairy conglomerate I told you about, the one who made the original offer, they're buying us out. The treks are finished."

Marnie had never heard Sam use that tone of voice before, and it scared her. It sounded like he'd just given up, like he just didn't care what happened anymore.

"Noooooooooo!" Her protest came out as a cross between a screech and a wail, as she tried to digest what Sam had just told her. "But you said... that money I gave you... we've been working so hard! No, Sam, you can't let this happen!"

"It has happened," he told her flatly. "That money bought us time, but weeks only. We just haven't had enough trekkers through the place to make the payments. If I don't accept this offer, which is actually pretty good, the bank is going to foreclose and we'll be forced to sell anyway. And we'll end up coming out with a whole lot less."

"But I don't want to go." Her voice was small, broken, just like her heart. She'd finally found somewhere she wanted to call home, and it was being ripped out from under her. Just like the earthquakes had done to her city—broken it down, destroyed dreams, left a path of destruction in its wake. And that's what the big dairy conglomerate would do here—devastation. They'd bulldoze the old house, no doubt. It needed so much work to bring it up to date that it would probably be cheaper to pull it down and start again. And the barn? That would probably be gone too, to make way for a cowshed. The round pen, the yards, the arena... all that would be demolished, to be replaced by a feed pad, tanker track, races. They'd put in an effluent pond, cut down all the trees. There would be no more horses, no more sheep, no more goats. No more anything, except cows. Stupid cows. On this huge farm there would be room for a lot of cows.

Sam set her on her feet but kept a hold of her, his palm cupping her chin, tilting her face up to look at him. "Neither do I, but we don't have a choice. Whether we sell now or later, either way, we're going to lose this place, and there isn't anything either of us can do about it."

"No. You're wrong." Her eyes filled with tears, blurring her vision.

"I'm not wrong. The deal's done, Marnie. I'll be signing the agreement and faxing it off this afternoon. After that, we'll have a month, at the most, to pack up our lives and get out of here."

Marnie wrenched her face out of Sam's grasp. She felt too insignificant with him holding her like that. And right now, she didn't want to feel insignificant. She was too upset to be insignificant. Straightening her shoulders, she stood on her tiptoes to make herself as tall as possible, which was still a heck of a lot shorter than Sam. "All we need is more time," she announced, as if this was the most obvious solution in the world.

"We don't have more time," Sam snapped. "Do you not think I've thought this through? We're out of options. Selling up is the only sensible thing to do."

"Fuck sensible! Sensible is for old boring people whose dreams have died."

"Our dreams have died," Sam murmured. He was most definitely not the crying type but right then, it sounded like he was about to. Marnie's heart clenched. Then Sam straightened up and frowned down at her. "And if you swear again, little girl, I'm going to cart you back off to the house and wash your mouth out with soap. Is that clear?"

A shiver went down Marnie's spine. She loved his stern dominance. Seeing him battling with his emotions and letting her get away with stuff she wouldn't ordinarily get away with, was almost as hard as hearing Sam tell her the place had been sold.

Sam raised an eyebrow. "I said, is that clear?"

Heat shot straight to Marnie's loins. "Yes, Daddy," she murmured. "But I still don't want to leave."

Sam put an arm around her shoulders and pulled her in close, kissing her forehead in that way she loved. "Neither do I. But the deal's as good as done. Let's just enjoy this trek, hey? You can come on this one. We'll go to the waterfall. It's a nice ride."

Tears burned the back of her eyes and blurred her vision. How was she going to saddle up horses when she couldn't see? Wiping them away with her sleeve was pointless because her eyes filled up again. Trixie knew something was up. As soon as she saw Marnie, she came trotting up to the fence, nickering, stretching her neck over the rails as far as it would go. Marnie went to her. Probably, Trixie would be one of the first to go. Her stomach clenched. She couldn't do this, couldn't say goodbye. Trixie was the first horse she'd been up close to, the first horse she'd really touched. She didn't want to leave her behind. Giggling through her tears, she kissed the outstretched velvety muzzle, squirming as Trixie's whiskers tickled her cheek. She'd miss this girl.

The ache in her heart worsened as she went about her chores. She should have been happy, mucking out stalls for probably the last time. Knowing she wouldn't have to shovel any more shit should have made her happy. But it didn't. She would clean up horse poo every day for the rest of her life, if it meant she got to stay here with Sam and he didn't have to sell up.

Tears streamed down her face as she gathered the brushes and hoof picks she would need to groom the horses before tacking them up. When she'd first arrived she'd been terrified of the big beasts, she was too scared to get too close, too afraid of their size to run a brush over their body. Now she loved it. She knew all their names, knew their different personalities. She knew Taxi would stand there no matter what, but Ranger hated his near fore hoof lifted up. She knew Cosmo liked to nuzzle her neck and would nip her if she didn't rub his nose enough, and she knew that Boxer would play up if he didn't have on the right bridle. What would happen to all these horses? Sam had already said he wouldn't be able to take them all.

She couldn't cry like this. Sam still needed her, and the least she could do was be professional one time before it all came to an end. Wiping her eyes, she carried the tools out to the horses who stood patiently as they had a hundred times before, and she started combing out Taxi's mane with a reverence she never imagined she'd feel working with a horse.

Sam was doing the same further down the line, his face set in a hard mask she knew was holding back a whole lot of emotion. The hollowness of it all kept resonating through her chest and belly. How could this be the end? It couldn't be the end.

"What's going to happen to them?" She risked the question, even though it made her choke up just to form the words.

"We'll keep a couple. The rest we'll have to sell."

"Sell?"

"I reckon we can get ten acres after everything is paid out," he said. "So we can have three or four there, but the rest will have to be sold to new riding homes. Can't have twenty horses on ten acres."

"Which ones will you sell?"

"I don't know," he sighed. "I haven't got that far yet."

"I don't want to sell any of them."

"I know," he said, his jaw clenched tight.

Marnie closed her mouth. She knew Sam was just as upset as she was. Probably a lot more. Blinking back tears, she did as she was told and got on with the job she'd never wanted for what might be the very last time.

CHAPTER ELEVEN

It had been a very long, brutally hard day. Sam was exhausted and he knew Marnie was too. After her initial outburst, she'd taken the news much better than he thought she would. Together, they'd taken a small band of tourists up along mountain plains and through the valleys and rivers he knew and loved so well.

It was hard to believe this was all coming to an end. Sam had been riding these lands since he was just a kid. They'd been in the family since the first settlers came to the South Island. And now it was over, eroded by time and a world that changed far faster than the old farm could ever have kept up with.

She'd scooted inside before he had a chance to talk to her, and he'd let her be. Now he was hungry, and in addition to getting some tea, he needed to finish signing those forms. He'd been putting it off, but it was inevitable now. If they wanted to claw back anything from the sale of the farm, they needed to take this offer.

He went to the table where he'd left the paperwork that morning. None of it was there. Frowning to himself, Sam hunted around for it. He even went out to the barn to check if he'd left the contracts out there. Nope. Couldn't find them anywhere. Weird.

He went back indoors and called up the stairs.

"Marnie?"

There was no response. Sam jogged up the stairs and checked the bedrooms as well as the bathroom. No Marnie. She was as mysteriously absent as the paperwork. Frowning to himself, he jogged back downstairs and went out the front and around the back of the house, calling for Marnie.

After about five minutes, she came out from behind the barn looking unmistakeably sheepish. She pushed something into the pocket of her jeans and put her hands behind her back as he got closer.

"What have you been doing, little girl?"

"Nothing," she lied to his face. They both knew it was a lie the moment she said the word. Sam gritted his teeth. Now really wasn't the time for her to start acting up, though of course it was almost inevitable that she would. This whole sale was going to be a nightmare on every level. Sam was determined not to let it come between him and Marnie, and he definitely wasn't going to let it affect his discipline of her.

"I'm looking for the contracts," he said. "Have you seen them?"

She hesitated for a moment and looked at the ground. "Yeah. I saw them this morning."

"I mean, have you seen them more recently?"

She shrugged.

Sam let out a growl, reached out and took her by the chin, tipping her head up so he could look into her disobedient little face.

"Where are those papers?"

"You're not signing them," she said, finding defiance in the forced eye contact.

"Little girl…"

"No," she said, trembling with defiance. "We're not giving this place up. We're not selling. You're not signing."

If only sheer determination could save the place, it

would be with them forever, but reality was biting hard and the truth was, the place had been failing since long before either of them had gotten there. It wasn't their fault that this was all falling apart any more than it had been Marnie's fault that her city fell apart. He was sorry she had to go through this again, not even a year after the quakes. She was going to be more unsettled than ever, and her behaviour was probably going to reflect that.

"What did you do with the contracts?"

Marnie looked him dead in the eye. "I burned them."

"You bloody what?" Sam released her jaw and stared at her.

"We're not selling, so I burned them."

"Marnie!" He shouldn't have been shocked, but he was. "You burned them?"

"Yeah," she said, folding her arms over her chest and tossing her hair. "I set them on fire and then they were burned and now the place isn't being sold, so I fixed the problem."

She wasn't this naive. She knew it wasn't going to work. It was the small, desperate part of her that had come up with a small, desperate plan to save Terako Treks.

"You know I'm just going to get them to send me another set of forms," he sighed.

"And I'll burn those too," Marnie said. "I'll burn everything I need to."

"Arson isn't the answer, little girl."

"Well, apparently working hard and trying everything I know how to do wasn't the answer either," she said bitterly. "So I'm just going with fire now. It's easier."

Again, he understood her frustration, but that didn't mean he was going to tolerate it. She was in big trouble. He reached out, took her by the hand, and started walking her toward the house. She traipsed after him reluctantly, knowing exactly what she was in for.

Just as they got into the house, the phone started to ring.

"I'm going to take this call, and then I'm going to take

my belt to your ass," he growled sternly, making for the kitchen where the old corded phone still hung on the wall.

"Yes? This is Sam Cooper."

• • • • • • •

She was in so much fucking trouble. Marnie knew burning the contracts wouldn't help, but it had felt so goddamn good to watch fire lick around the edges of those dreaded papers and then consume the horrible typewritten text that represented the end of her life here with Sam.

Whoever was on the phone had only given her a very brief reprieve. That belt around his waist was thick and mean, and Sam sure had a hell of a lot of frustration to work out on her rear.

Marnie thought briefly about running away, but it was pointless. He'd just catch her and then whip her and that would be even worse than what was going to come anyway. She wasn't sorry for what she'd done though, and she would do it again if she got the chance.

She'd been working so damn hard to increase the visibility of the place, taking out online ads, making pages, emailing websites; hell, she'd even uploaded Sam's shirtless whip tricks, though that was more a brag than anything. There weren't many women who could boast having a man like Sam. She was damn proud of him, even if he was going to put that incredible musculature to use punishing her very soon.

Standing nervously in the corner of the kitchen, Marnie watched Sam's expression go from angry to confused to cautious... and then a big, broad smile broke over his face.

"Well, that sounds perfect," he said. "Can't wait to meet you. Talk soon."

He hung up and looked at her with that grin that made her heart leap for a dozen different reasons. "Well, little girl," he said with a smirk. "Seems you've been up to quite a lot I don't know about."

"Uhm, like what?"

"Apparently some video you posted online has been seen over ten million times. It's trending? I don't know what that means, but that was an investor. Someone who wants to not only help us keep this place, but update it."

Marnie's jaw dropped. "Are you serious?"

"Mhm. We're going to meet with the group's representatives soon," he said. "If it all works out, we might just get to keep this place after all—assuming you don't burn it down first."

"Oh, my god, Sam!" Marnie screamed his name at a pitch pretty close to what only dogs could hear and threw herself into his arms. "We get to stay?"

"We get to stay, little girl," he confirmed, drawing her into a big bear hug. "We at least get another chance to stay."

His palm ran down her back and his fingers spread across her ass. "You did it, Marnie. If this works out, you saved Terako."

"We did it," she said with a teary grin. "I couldn't have done it without posting semi-naked pictures of you on the internet."

"You did what now?" Sam jerked his head back and looked down at her. "Are you serious, Marnie?"

"Well, you were wearing pants," she grinned. "I mean, it was soft-core at best."

"Little girl, you are the worst brat in the world, and the best woman any man could ever have by his side," he declared, kissing her deeply. "And now, I'm going to spank this little ass of yours."

"Hey, not fair!"

"Very fair," he said sternly. "Even good little girls deserve spankings, and you're pretty far from a good little girl."

"I'm the best little girl," Marnie declared.

And she was right.

EPILOGUE

"Ready? Now!" Ensuring the camera was firmly in its tripod, Marnie pressed 'play' and watched, both proud and aroused, as Sam's handsome body danced in time to the music. The muscles in his back and shoulders rippled as he cracked his whips, one in each hand.

Crack, crack, crack, crack. His hips moved in time with the beat, the swivelling motion spreading through his body, as his biceps flexed with the exertion of cracking the whip.

Since the viral video that had saved Terako, Sam had become an internet sensation. Their YouTube channel had thousands of subscribers, along with the Facebook page and Instagram, and the website Marnie had set up had thousands of hits every day. Thanks to Sam and his sexy shirtless whip-cracking skills, Terako was busier than ever. So busy in fact, that it was hard to find the time between treks to film. And while there was plenty Marnie could and did do—everything from updating all the social media to mucking out stalls, and even leading a few shorter treks—there were some things, like this, she needed Sam for. No matter how hard she tried she couldn't crack a whip. And even if she succeeded she'd never be in Sam's class and she'd never ever in a million years look as good as he did without a shirt on.

Marnie had got the idea of Sam cracking a whip to music from something she'd seen online—an Australian guy had done it, and it had been the hottest thing she'd seen. She'd mentioned it to Sam, and now he had a whole repertoire of songs he liked to use, mostly stuff that was older than she was. Leaning back against the fence, she watched, totally enthralled, as Sam cracked his whips in time to the beat of 'Achy Breaky Heart.'

Relaxing in the sunshine, Marnie couldn't keep herself from smiling. They had come a long way. When he'd first seen the video of him that had gone viral, he'd hit the roof. He'd been mortified, and her backside had paid a heavy price. But then when he'd calmed down and read the comments, mostly of adulation from scores of admiring women, he'd decided that maybe she was onto something. Now, as often as possible, they filmed something new. And it was working. Terako Treks was the biggest, most well-known trekking place in the country, and they took out tourists from all over the world. It seemed that everyone wanted to see the shirtless whip cracker in action. Sam was famous. And he was hers. Sometimes, she still had to pinch herself to believe it.

The song ended; Marnie turned off the camera. The instant she turned her back to Sam, she felt the leather thong of his whip wrap around her waist.

"Come here, little girl," he growled, his voice a gruff tone of authority. A tingle went down Marnie's spine. She loved the sound of his voice, especially when he pretended that she was in trouble and injected a stern note into it.

"Have I told you lately how much I love you?" Tugging on the whip, he pulled her in toward him. Heat shot to her core as he bent down to kiss her nose.

"Nope, you haven't," Marnie insisted. "Not today, anyway."

With a flick of his wrist, the whip unwrapped itself from around Marnie and dropped to the ground.

"I've got to tell you something," he said, his voice

dropping into a low timbre.

"What?" Marnie frowned a little as his arms replaced the whip in drawing her close to him. She hoped it wasn't something bad. There had been enough trouble to last them a long time, but she still worried a little every day that something might still go wrong.

"We've done it, little girl," he whispered in her ear, hugging her tight. "Terako Treks is mortgage-free. It's ours. Forever."

A squeal of pure joy escaped Marnie as he bent her back over his arm, her head dipping toward the ground as he literally swept her off her feet.

She flung her arms around his neck and squealed with shock. "Sam! Put me down!"

"Not a chance, little girl. Now shut up and kiss me."

THE END

Made in the USA
Middletown, DE
21 May 2019